"You're Living A Lie, Logan Claiborne, And I'm One Of The Few People Who Knows It. You're No Elegant, Refined Gentleman. You Use Your Money Like A Shield To Fend Off Anything That's Real…Like Me."

"Do the smart thing for once. Just leave."

"Or you'll what?" When she licked her mouth, making her lower lip shine wetly, something that had been wound too tight for nine damn years snapped inside him, unleashing a force he would have denied with every breath in his body.

With a suddenness that startled them both, his hard arms circled her and then crushed her against him. "You shouldn't have come back here. You shouldn't have messed with me again."

"So, you *do* want me…a little," she whispered, her musical voice a husky taunt against his throat. "Is that why you're so afraid of me?"

Yes, she was right. He wanted her naked and writhing underneath him again.

Dear Reader,

For me, there is something romantic about Louisiana. When I lived on the Sabine River, I loved to drive over from Texas to visit that state. I fell in love with its past; with its French culture and Southern traditions; with its slow-moving bayous and fauna; with the Cajuns' fun-loving spirit; with the African-Americans' jazz and swamp pop. My husband is still sad that he can't really hear swamp pop played in south Texas where we now reside. Oh, and Louisiana has great food!

I have enjoyed visiting the old plantation homes along the River Road and reading the diaries of the families who lived there. It always distresses me that in the fast-paced modern world, it is so difficult to preserve these windows into the past. When Katrina struck Louisiana, much was lost.

With my longtime fascination for this state and its stories, I suppose it's only natural that I was inspired to set my latest series in Louisiana.

Vicariously, as I write this series, I will get to return to this lovely place that will always haunt me.

All my best,

Ann Major

ANN MAJOR

TO TAME HER TYCOON LOVER

Silhouette® Desire

Published by Silhouette Books

America's Publisher of Contemporary Romance

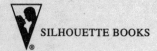 SILHOUETTE BOOKS

Recycling programs
for this product may
not exist in your area.

ISBN-13: 978-0-373-76984-1

TO TAME HER TYCOON LOVER

Copyright © 2009 by Ann Major

Visit Silhouette Books at www.eHarlequin.com

Printed in U.S.A.

ANN MAJOR

lives in Texas with her husband of many years and is the mother of three grown children. She has a master's degree from Texas A&M at Kingsville, Texas, and is a former English teacher. She is a founding board member of the Romance Writers of America and a frequent speaker at writers' groups.

Ann loves to write; she considers her ability to do so a gift. Her hobbies include hiking in the mountains, sailing, ocean kayaking, traveling and playing the piano. But most of all she enjoys her family. Visit her Web site at www.annmajor.com.

I dedicate this book to Krista Stroever, my editor. I loved writing this book because the characters and their story were so keenly alive for me. That said, her editing made this novel far better than it would have been without her. Many thanks, Krista.

One

Some women are impossible to forget no matter how a man tries.

Logan Claiborne was frowning, and not because the sun was in his eyes as he sped down the narrow, twisting road that led to the antebellum mansion where he'd grown up.

He should be concentrating on Mitchell Butler and the merger of Butler Shipyards and Claiborne Energy, or on how he was going to deal compassionately with Grandpère once he arrived at Belle Rose.

Instead, his grip tightened on the steering wheel as he remembered the open, trusting, dark eyes of the voluptuously proportioned swamp brat he'd seduced and then jilted nine years ago to save his twin brother, Jake.

Until this morning, Logan had told himself that his grandfather had been right, that Cici Bellefleur didn't belong in their world; that he'd had to save Jake from the same sort of disastrous marriage their father had made to a poor girl, *their* mother, whose extravagant dreams of grandeur as well as her need to impress had nearly wrecked the family fortune. He'd continued to tell himself that he'd been right to do what he'd done even after he'd secured the family empire, even after Cici had made a name for herself with her camera and had proved herself a woman of talent and worth.

Then his grandfather had called him this morning and had stunned him by acting as thrilled as an infatuated kid when he'd mentioned Cici had come home again and they were giving tours of the house together.

Why had she, a famous photographer and writer, really come home? What did she want?

"Nine years ago you were dead set against her because of her uncle," Logan had reminded him. Grand-père had always distrusted Cici's uncle.

"In a long life, a man makes a few mistakes. Remember that. I made more than a few. Someday you may have a stroke that leaves you with too much time to dwell on the past. You may regret some of the things you've done. Well, I regret blaming Cici for her uncle Bos. It wasn't her fault he fought cocks, ran with a wild bunch and operated a bar."

"Do you remember that nine years ago you didn't want her anywhere near Jake or me, *especially* Jake, who was running pretty wild back then?"

"Well, I'm sorry for that, if I did."

"If you did?" It was still difficult to reconcile the grandfather he had now with the domineering individual who had raised him.

"Okay, I was wrong about her. I was wrong to be so tough on you, too. It's my fault you're so hard."

A pang of guilt had hit Logan as he'd run his hand through his rumpled, chocolate-brown hair.

"I was too hard on Jake, too."

"Maybe you're being too difficult on yourself."

"I'd like to see Jake again before I die."

"You're not going to die…not anytime soon."

"Cici says the same thing. She thinks I'm getting better every day. She thinks maybe I could stay here instead of…" His voice trailed away.

The mention of Cici and the hope in his grandfather's voice had convinced Logan he had to check on his grandfather at once. Since his stroke, his grandfather had gone from being a strong, commanding man to a clingy, depressed person Logan barely knew. This was why Logan had decided his grandfather couldn't live independently at Belle Rose any longer and needed to be moved to New Orleans near him. The old man needed looking after.

Unfortunately, the dense forest with its vines and wild vegetation was so thick beneath the brooding sky,

Logan was almost past the familiar turn to his childhood home before he saw the gatepost. At the last moment, he spun the wheel of his Lexus to the right too fast and skidded. No sooner had he righted the car than he saw the pillared mansion at the end of the oak alley. As always, the ancient home with its graceful columns and galleries aglow in the slanting sunlight seemed to him the most beautiful of houses, claiming his heart as no other place could.

How could he blame Grandpère, who'd become more childlike and emotional since his debilitating illness, for wanting to stay here? Logan remembered the first time he had mentioned the possibility of moving him to the city. Grandpère had given him a scare by disappearing for several hours.

Cici has no business convincing the old man he's getting better so he'll think he doesn't have to move.

But was that really her motivation?

The mere thought of his grandfather's worsening condition was upsetting. Logan, not Cici, had Grandpère's best interests at heart. The last thing he needed was Cici meddling and making him feel guilty about a decision he'd been forced to make. He didn't want to make Grandpère unhappy, but he couldn't run Claiborne Energy and be down here with his grandfather at the same time.

His thoughts in a snarl, Logan braked too sharply. His tires spun in the damp gravel as he stopped in the deep shade beneath the wide alley of the spreading oaks some anonymous Frenchman had planted a hundred years before the antebellum house had even been dreamed of. Beyond the house, fields stretched to a line of brooding cypress trees draped with moss that edged the wilderness of the swamp.

Logan flung the gleaming door of his late-model Lexus hybrid open and stepped out of the luxury sedan. After having his tall frame jammed behind the wheel for the two hour drive over bad roads from New Orleans, it felt good to stand up and stretch.

Despite the huge live oak trees, the heat was unbearably steamy for this early in March. He inhaled the thick, syrupy air, which to him smelled of home.

Little green frogs croaked. Bees hummed in azalea blossoms. Wood ducks made music. Did he only imagine lusty bull alligators roaring for their mates?

He smiled. How Cici used to love the dark, moss-hung wilderness that bordered the plantation when she'd been a kid. Whenever he'd been home and had put a foot outside, she'd followed him everywhere as eagerly as a devoted puppy. Their relationship had been so simple then. She'd been eight years younger than he and Jake, so Logan hadn't taken her crush on his brother seriously until the summer he'd returned home from law school and discovered that his grandfather was right about Cici not being a child any longer.

Shutting his mind against those pleasant memories that included Cici, he began to regret he was out of the air-conditioned car.

Maybe because he dreaded seeing Cici so much, Logan took the time to rip his tie off and unbutton his collar. Shedding his custom-made suit jacket, he opened the door and tossed his jacket and tie onto his plush, leather seat.

He wished Alicia Butler, his girlfriend of the past four months, had been able to come with him. Maybe then he wouldn't feel so haunted by the past. Or so tempted to remember Cici.

Unlike Cici, Alicia was sleek and elegant. He'd met her because they'd been thrown together due to his ambition to merge his company with her father's. A brunette, her shoulder-length, straight hair made her slim face seem even more regal. She knew how to dress, how to carry herself. Heads turned at fundraisers whenever she was at his side, and not only because of her beauty and stylish attire, but because of her fortune.

Other men, ambitious men, envied him. Not that that was the only reason he felt such a sense of pride that she would soon be his.

Poised, she approached life deliberately, as he did. She was civilized, polished and, therefore, as appropriate for him as his wife, Noelle, had been before her untimely death.

Alicia spoke French and Italian. She set a beautiful table. She never ate too much or drank too much or wore an inappropriate outfit.

Not even when she was angry did she raise her voice. She was equally controlled in bed, too.

As Cici had not been, sprang the wayward thought. For an instant his blood pounded as he remembered Cici wild with pleasure, writhing beneath him.

But Alicia would warm up after they were married. He would be patient. He understood not trusting enough to ever let go. Together he and Alicia would build a life together as he and Noelle, his recently departed wife, had, a life that everyone would envy. They wouldn't quarrel horribly and tear each other to pieces because their passions got in the way.

Briefly he remembered Noelle's sad eyes in that last week before she'd died. Then, quickly as always, he ruthlessly checked the forbidden image. He *would* make Alicia happy. History would not repeat itself.

"I'm sorry I can't come with you and meet your grandfather, darling," Alicia had said when he'd called her this morning. "But Daddy needs me at the office."

"Okay. I understand."

Mitchell Butler, Alicia's father, was a domineering shark, at least in business, but since Logan and he had this huge merger between their businesses pending, Logan didn't want to cross him over something as minor as a personal issue. He would see Alicia tonight.

"Darling, I'm sure you'll know exactly what to say and do to make your grandfather understand why he may not be able to stay at Belle Rose," Alicia had said. "After all, it's *your* family. He's your grandfather. You love him and want only the best for him."

If she only knew what a mess he'd made of things,

Logan thought grimly. He'd made everybody unhappy. His family remained divided, as a result.

He didn't want to dwell on his mistakes, especially not on his brutal handling of Cici the first time around or his nine-year estrangement from his twin. His thoughts on damage control and what was best for his grandfather, Logan had rushed down here today despite his heavy schedule. He was determined to deal with Cici before she got creative and made his grandfather believe he could have the impossible.

He remembered how small and lost Cici had looked standing on the dock after he'd told her he didn't love her. He'd lied to protect her and him. Strangely, his lie had made him feel equally sad.

Don't think about the past. Or how you felt. Just deal with Cici now.

Despite his best intentions not to revisit the past, he remembered young, vivacious Cici trying to pretend she was strong and tough and as good as the rich and powerful Claibornes. He'd hurt her. Hurt Jake. Hurt everybody, including himself. And told himself it was collateral damage because the family was richer and stronger than ever.

After locking the car, Logan turned and strode up the gravel drive toward the softly glowing house. But at the base of the stairs that led to the lower gallery and massive front door, he paused.

Slowly his gaze drifted over the mansion and lawn. A newly built wooden wheelchair ramp that avoided the stairs snaked back and forth from the ground to the front door.

Logan's eyes roved over the familiar grounds, out to the *garçonnière* where he and Jake had lived as teenagers before their quarrel over Cici, and he wondered who owned the two-seater Miata parked at such a jaunty angle beside the building.

Frowning, he made for the stairs, but just as he was about to turn the knob and push at the front door, it was opened by someone inside the house.

"Why, hello there, Mister Logan," said the soft, familiar, French-accented voice of his childhood nanny.

Noonoon, his grandfather's housekeeper now, stood just inside the big door. At the sight of him, her dark face lit up as brightly as a birthday cake.

An answering warmth filled him. This generous-hearted woman had always loved him, loved Jake, too. Ever since their mother's death, she'd practically run Belle Rose single-handedly.

"Lordy, it shore is a hot day."

He nodded, gave her a quick hug, then released her.

"Come on in out of the heat before you melt. If it's this hot now, what'll it be like in August?"

"Don't get me started about August." Because of the gulf heating up in the summer, August was a prime month for hurricanes.

"Can I fix you something? A drink maybe? Iced tea with a sprig of mint?"

He shook his head. "I'm fine."

"You shore are. At thirty-five, you're as tall and handsome as ever."

"Why do you remind me of my age every chance you get?"

"Maybe because it's time you stopped grieving so hard for your pretty Miss Noelle."

He tensed.

She stopped, realizing he wasn't the sort to encourage sympathy. "Life is short," she said.

"I have someone new in my life." He stepped into the welcoming cool of the wide central hall. "Her name's Alicia Butler. You'll meet her soon. She's a real lady. Someone the family will be proud of."

Noonoon shut the door behind him. "I'm real glad. So, what brings you all the way down here from New Orleans?"

"My grandfather. He's so deaf he's hard to talk to over the phone. I thought we had things settled, but this morning he was saying he was better and wanted to stay here on his own." Deliberately Logan refrained from mentioning Cici.

"Mr. Pierre, he be napping upstairs. But he'll be mighty pleased, he will…that you're here…since we don't see much of you these days, you bein' such a busy, important man and all and living in New Orleans."

"Napping? Where is *she*, then?" Logan asked.

"Miss Cici?" Noonoon inquired a little too innocently.

Logan nodded. "Who else?"

"I knew it wouldn't take you long…as soon as you heard about Miss Cici. There shore isn't nothing like a rich older man taking an interest in a beautiful, younger woman for getting the rest of his family's hackles up, now is there?"

"That's not why…"

Her intelligent, black eyes regarding him intently, Noonoon placed her hands on her wide hips. So, Cici had already won Noonoon over.

"When you heard about Miss Cici, you come down here faster than that lazy hare sprinting at the last second to catch that tortoise in that story I used to read to you two boys. Why, I'll never forget that last summer she was here. Miss Cici, I mean. She was eighteen and just the prettiest little thing I ever saw."

Logan wished to hell he couldn't remember the way slanting sunlight had washed Cici's breasts with light and shadow as she'd stood in her pirogue the first day he'd come home. When she'd seen him, she'd jumped out of the boat and had run into the woods, her long legs flying gracefully. When he'd followed her, she'd said hi and her dark eyes had sparkled with such joy, she'd bewitched him. After that, she'd been too shy to say more, and, hell, so had he.

Logan's eyes narrowed, and Noonoon changed tack.

"She only be here a week, Miss Cici, and Mr. Pierre, he already plum crazy about her."

"He told me," Logan said coldly, imagining Cici preying on the vulnerable old man.

"He been doing real good. I know you wants him to move to New Orleans and all…"

"To a fabulous assisted living arrangement near my house that I can personally supervise."

"But places like that aren't home, and we all know how busy you be. How often could you get yourself over to see him? Mr. Pierre, he be happy here. Old people at those homes just sit and stare."

"You can't take care of him day and night. You have your own family."

Since the house was open to the public, Noonoon's main job was as a housekeeper, not a caregiver to his grandfather. She'd agreed to help with him temporarily.

"Well, now that Miss Cici is here…"

"She's not staying."

"Well, she sing and play the piano for him every day. She talk to him. Most nights they eat dinner together. She cooks. You remember how she loves to cook."

"The way she runs around all over the world, she won't be here that long."

"You sure about that? She shore is settlin' in. Says she's tired of all that running, that she's had enough pain to last her a lifetime. And she have her book to write."

"Not another book. I hope she's focusing on something that has nothing to do with me this time."

"She hasn't mentioned you."

He wasn't reassured. Cici's book on the oil industry in Louisiana after Katrina had made Claiborne Energy look bad. Had she mentioned even once how many people had jobs because of Claiborne Oil? No, her book had been full of pictures of rusting pipelines and oil-covered wildlife and shots of boats on water that used to be land with captions blaming companies like Claiborne Energy for the state's vanishing marshlands.

"And she wants to see about her uncle Bos and all," Noonoon was saying. "He's not too strong, you know, after his treatments. Stubborn cuss, though. She calls and calls him, but he still won't speak to her. You'd think after all these years, he'd forgive her. All she ever did was be friends with you and Jake."

Guilt made a muscle in his jaw pull. So, she was still estranged from her uncle. Just like he and Jake were estranged from each other…because of that summer. Not that most decent people in these parts thought Bos was worth knowing. Still, he was her uncle. He'd taken her in when she was orphaned.

Bos and Grandpère's enmity had sharpened over the issue of Bos's cockfighting. Once fighting cocks had become illegal, the two had had fewer issues to quarrel over.

"Cici said she wants to live somewhere quiet, and you of all people know the *garçonnière* is mighty quiet."

"You gave her the *garçonnière?* My old rooms?" He was shouting, and he never shouted. Not even when someone as hard as Mitchell Butler tried to screw Claiborne Energy for millions.

"Mr. Pierre, he be the one who rent it to her," she defended herself softly.

Remembering the cute red Miata parked by the two-story octagonal building, Logan's pulse began to thud. So, the dangerous, flashy sports car was hers. Why was that a surprise? Cici had a reckless streak. And no wonder…with that trapper cockfighting, swamp-rat of an uncle who'd raised her, mainly by neglecting her.

If his grandfather had been himself he would know that Cici couldn't be dedicated to him in any real way. No, she probably had some secret agenda.

"Sorry I raised my voice," Logan whispered, straining for control. "This isn't your fault. Or hers. It's mine— for not moving Grandpère sooner. I'll deal with her now."

"Oh, Miss Cici, she don't like anybody bothering her in the afternoon. Not unless it's an emergency. You see, she writes when Mr. Pierre naps. Then at four she and Mr. Pierre, they give the last tour together. I reckon she be free to talk around five."

"How can he manage walking so far in his condition?"

Noonoon's sharp look made him wince as he remembered he hadn't seen his grandfather in a month.

"Miss Cici got him off his walker. Gave him a cane and bought him a new, lightweight wheelchair. She hired Mr. Buzz to build ramps everywhere. She pushes Pierre when he be tired. With the ramps he can get up to all the slave cabins now."

More ramps? Logan's pulse in his temple had speeded up. He didn't believe Cici had come home to care for his grandfather. She had never known how to take proper care of herself. No way could she take care of Pierre. Not for the long haul.

His grandfather needed dedicated nurses and the latest, modern, long-term care, and he was going to have them.

More to the point: his grandfather was his responsibility.

The sooner he dealt with Cici and sent her packing, the better.

Two

Cici turned off the hot water and sighed. For the first time in a long time, she felt good, surprisingly good. Almost at peace with herself.

Maybe taking a break from her cameras and all the death she'd seen in war zones and coming home had been the right decision after all.

She stepped out of the shower, grabbed a towel from the rack and flung it on the floor. Planting her bare feet with their hot pink nails on the thick terry cloth, she sucked in a breath and savored the sensual feel of warm water rushing down her breasts and belly and thighs onto the towel.

Her toes curled into the soft terry in sheer delight. She,

who'd lived for months in tents with no running water, appreciated a hot shower in a safe, familiar locale as the luxuries they truly were. Whipping a second towel free, she wound it around her curly, wet hair and began to rub.

The windows were open. The sweetness of the faint breeze that brought the scents of magnolia and crepe myrtle and pine through the second-story windows caused her to shiver.

Frogs sang. No, they roared in chorus right along with the bull alligators after the rain last night when she'd taken Pierre's pirogue and had paddled it out into the brooding swamp to watch the herons and egrets and buzzards flying home to their nests.

She squeezed her eyes shut and listened. She could almost hear the stirring of moss in the cypress trees.

"Aah," she murmured, sighing heavily and yet very happily. She knew she was procrastinating, that she should be at the computer writing, but she couldn't resist taking a moment to appreciate fully the bliss of being home after years of exile.

Writers had so many excuses for not writing. Life versus work was a biggie. How could you write if you did not let yourself experience life?

Content to procrastinate, she took in a deep breath and then another. Until this particular, miraculous moment, for such moments of true awareness were small miracles, she'd never let herself admit how much she'd longed to come home and see Belle Rose again. For always, always Belle Rose, ever since she'd been orphaned at eight and brought to live in her Uncle Bos's shack on marshy land that bordered the Claibornes' superior property Belle Rose had stood like a vision of paradise in her imagination.

There was no place for her at Belle Rose, yet she'd always wanted to belong. The closest she'd ever come to that had been when Uncle Bos had worked briefly as a part-time gardener for the Claibornes, and she'd had free run of the place. That's when she'd formed the habit of following Logan everywhere any time he was home.

"What the hell?" the deep, too-familiar voice of the present master of Belle Rose roared as lustily as any bull alligator.

For a second or two she felt the same rush of adrenaline in her stomach she'd known when that bullet in Afghanistan had whizzed by her face, missing her by mere inches.

You had to get close to death to film it.

She opened her eyes, and when they fastened on the tall, broad-shouldered man, who was in her bedroom, she screamed.

For nine years she'd imagined what clever thing she'd say or do if she ever saw Logan Claiborne again. She'd give him a piece of her mind, for one thing. But in this long, nightmarish moment, she just stood where she was like a dumbstruck idiot. Vaguely she noted that his eyes were as wide with conflicting emotions as hers probably were.

If he'd taken a single step toward her or said something clever and belittling, she would have screamed again. But since he was as paralyzed as she, she did nothing. Absolutely nothing.

She just stood there without a stitch on and let him gape at her. For the record, and she being a journalist kept minute records, a whirlwind of thoughts and feelings and visual images did storm through her. At first, they flew so fast and hard she couldn't focus on any particular memory. Still, for a second or two she felt keenly in touch with her younger, more vulnerable self—that naive, innocent eighteen-year-old girl who'd loved him, trusted him and had been shattered by his callous treatment.

How could he have misused her so? They'd grown up together. She'd always had a crush on Jake, his wilder twin. Logan had been more like a brother to her, the brother who'd mainly ignored her but with whom she'd felt safe and comfortable around because no powerful childish crush got in the way and had made her shy around him.

He'd played in the swamp with her when she'd been a child. He'd taught her to tease alligators, collect egret feathers, trap crawfish. Then they'd grown up, and she'd given up her infatuation for Jake and had fallen in love with Logan. Hadn't he really, always been her hero? Then he'd made his move, and soon after, her fantasy world had come crashing down around her.

In this very room, or at least the bedroom where he stood, she'd lain naked beneath Logan, warmed by his larger body, never guessing he'd made love to her to save his brother. For an instant those fleeting, pulsing moments of cherished togetherness after he'd taken her virginity became too vividly real, stinging her with raw pain and fresh heartbreak all over again. All through those long summer nights, he'd made love to her again and again.

Every night she'd waited for Bos to go to his bar. Then she'd run through the woods to the *garçonnière*. She'd felt so piercingly alive in Logan's arms. And every night their passion had built.

She'd believed he'd loved her—until that last night when Jake had found them together and Logan had told her why he'd really slept with her—to save Jake from making a misalliance. Then Logan had walked out on her, and her fairy tale had ended.

For days she'd believed he'd come back and tell her he was sorry, tell her he loved her. How little she'd known back then of men.

When she'd called him two months later in the fall to talk, before she could tell him her news, he'd silenced her by coldly informing her he'd married Noelle.

She'd needed to talk to him. She'd felt so alone when she'd hung up the phone knowing she had to face a difficult situation by herself. So abandoned. Because of him, for years she'd hated all men, especially him.

At some point, she'd quit blaming men in general for his crimes, but she'd clung to her intense dislike of him.

But the shock of seeing him like this, with his cold, blue, too-adult eyes burning every part of her body, from her pert nipples to the soft, damp brush of gold between her legs, was so powerful, even her hatred could not compare.

Finally, she regained enough presence of mind to remember her towel. Scowling at him, she leaned down to get it and wrapped it around her with jerky, big movements, making sure she covered the moon-shaped scar on her abdomen first.

Even so, when she looked up, guiltily, warily, she found his male eyes still blazing too hotly with the unwanted memory of her naked body, and his gaze made her own nerves buzz. But covering herself only seemed to intensify the raw, unwanted intimacy between them.

Blushing while fighting not to remember those hot summer nights they'd shared in this very bedroom, she swallowed and tried to make her voice fierce and defiant. "You should have knocked, damn you."

"I did."

"Then you should have waited until I answered."

"Yes," he agreed, finally having the decency to look away. His gaze drifted over her desk that was littered with papers and index cards and photographs, some of him. "I should have."

A flush of dark color climbed his cheeks when he saw the newspaper clippings of his own ravaged face. The shot, which he couldn't stop staring at, had been taken shortly after Noelle's death.

Why, oh why did I leave that particular picture out?

"I didn't think," he said. "I never thought you'd be…"

"Nude?"

His angry blue gaze snapped back to her face. "Why didn't you lock the door? And how could you just stand there…flaunting yourself, like you liked me seeing you."

"Stop right there!" Heat engulfed her and not the good, soothing kind. This fire was a fury that devoured her.

"Damn you! This is not my fault! Nothing is my fault! You barged in here! And because you did, you found me stepping out of my shower, as I have every right to do…"

"Yes, I'm sorry. You're right!"

"I'm not finished. For your information, I've been taking showers these nine years since I last saw you! And nobody else, not even in a war zone, has ever barged in on me! You're in the wrong—not me."

"Okay. So you said…repeatedly. Enough already."

"No. It's not enough. You were horrible to me in the past. You're horrible now. You always act high and mighty because as far as you're concerned, I'll be poor white trash till the day I die. I wasn't good enough for Jake or you…and nothing I ever do will change that."

He swallowed. The muscle that moved in his jawline when he was upset jumped violently. "All right. I hear you. You made your point."

She most certainly had, but since he still hadn't bothered to apologize, she felt consumed by smoldering heat and indignation…and by other awful emotions she didn't want to name. How could he still affect her like this?"

Despite her discomfiture, his changed appearance registered. Not that she hadn't seen pictures of him in magazines and newspapers and on the Internet from time to time. He was a rich, important man. His wife's tragic accident and funeral alone had received a vast amount of coverage last year, all of which Cici had hungrily devoured.

Still, it was different, seeing him this close, knowing his anger was partly due to the fact that he wanted to be done with her, just as she wanted to be done with him.

She assessed him coldly. No longer was he the wiry boy she'd loved or even the gray-faced man in the photograph on her desks whose obvious grief had almost made her feel sorry for him. He'd filled out. And he'd grown, as men often do, even more virile and attractive than ever.

He was close-shaven. He wore an expensive white shirt that was so damp from the heat that it clung to his muscular body in such a way that she couldn't help admiring that he'd kept himself in shape.

He'd rolled up the sleeves, revealing strong, tanned forearms. His chocolate-brown hair might be shorter, but it still looked as thick and sexily tousled as ever.

To all who didn't know better, Logan appeared a respectable, wealthy businessman. But she, who wished she didn't know better, knew the wildness and the dangerous darkness that lurked beneath that suave, too-handsome exterior. Like herself, Logan didn't mind the edgy thrill of risk.

With an effort she reminded herself that Logan Claiborne was utterly self-serving and ruthless, and a smart woman would avoid him.

Still, he looked good. Too good. And not just because she hadn't dated anybody for a while.

Uncle Bos had been right about a few things. He'd said rich people could be crueler and colder than anybody, that she'd best stay away from the Claibornes and their like. "You're swamp trash to them. You're nothing more than a toy to play with. They throw girls like you to the sharks when they're through."

"Get out," she said quietly and yet forcefully.

He crossed his arms across his broad chest and spread his legs in a masculine, stubborn stance.

"Not till we talk," he said.

"If you think I'm going to stand here wearing only a towel and converse with you like nothing happened… after…after the way you barged in here, after the way you looked at me and accused me, you're crazy."

"Get dressed, then." He turned his broad shoulders to her. When she didn't move, he said calmly, "I won't watch. I promise."

"*As if!* As if I'd ever trust the likes of you again!"

He whirled, his blue eyes stormy when he faced her again. "Trust doesn't even enter into it. You're not staying at Belle Rose. Not one more night. You're going to leave my grandfather alone. He's vulnerable and old, easy prey…"

"Stop right there! For your information, I have a three-month lease and a publishing deadline to meet. And *your* grandfather, whom you claim to care so much about, was starving for affection. Starving. And I think I know something about how that condition feels—especially where you're concerned." She paused. "So, his needing me and befriending me when I came home feeling lonely and vulnerable and a bit alienated from my roots is a big part of why I have no intention of moving."

"You're just using him."

"And you know that, how, you who could write a book on that subject?" She took a deep breath. "Get out of my apartment, or I'm calling the law."

"This is Louisiana. I own the law. And since I didn't sign your lease, it isn't worth the paper it's written on. Now get dressed, so we can settle this once and for all. I'll wait downstairs."

"I'm not the same foolish girl I was nine years ago. You can't stomp in here and intimidate me."

"I will reimburse you every penny you've paid my grandfather and then some."

"Money. You think you can buy your way out of any problem."

"That's unfair, and you know it."

"Who just said, 'This is Louisiana. I own the law?'"

His dark face turned a mottled shade of purple that wasn't nearly so lovely on him as it was on the purple water hyacinths that choked the bayou at the edge of the lush grass behind Belle Rose.

"I'll wait for you on the gallery of Belle Rose," he managed, his posture stiff, his deep tone icy.

"I won't be allowed inside the house then?"

"You're the one putting yourself down," he said. "Not me."

"I own the law," she mocked.

When he stalked out without bothering to reply, she resisted the very strong impulse to slam the door. After letting it shut softly, she leaned against it for a long moment and tried to catch her breath.

She couldn't believe she'd been so rude. Even to him.

Did he ask for it, or what? Why did women with a drop of Southern blood always think they were supposed to be nice? Even to total jerks, which he was, even if he was rich and handsome and had a home like Belle Rose that was architectural poetry?

She moved away from the door toward her desk. Slowly she lifted the photograph of him where he looked so lost and sad. She'd taken so many pictures of people in pain, she recognized real suffering when she saw it.

Not wanting to think about that or to feel sorry for him, she slipped his picture inside a drawer.

Suddenly it dawned on her that she hadn't heard him stomp down the stairs. Was he standing on the other side of the door?

Or was he as upset and confused as she was after seeing her again?

Was he human after all?

When she considered the possibility that she might have hurt him, even just a little, she felt a strange catch in her heart just like she had when she'd first seen that picture of him after Noelle's death.

Closing her eyes, she saw his dark, pain-ravaged face after he'd told her making love to her had meant nothing…that he'd never loved her, that he'd only done it to save his twin. She'd never known which to believe: his brutal words or his heartbroken eyes.

She took a breath and told herself his jilting her was all that mattered. Like photographs, actions told the deepest truths.

When she removed her towel to dress, she caught sight of her reflection in the tall mirror on the wall.

Turning on the light, she studied the crescent-shaped scar on her stomach for a long moment. And as always, whenever she let herself remember that terrible night when she'd had an emergency C-section, the night she'd lost their baby son, fathered by a man who'd refused to even listen to her when she'd tried to tell him she was pregnant, she froze.

Under no circumstances could she allow herself to soften toward Logan Claiborne.

Grabbing a blouse, she turned away from the mirror. The last thing she needed was any reminder of how deeply involved she'd once been with the angry man who'd just left.

She was through with him forever.

Three

Logan was furious at himself for storming into the *garçonnière* after becoming impatient when Cici hadn't opened the door the minute he'd knocked.

Furious at her, too. How could she have just stood in her bathroom naked like that, smelling so sweetly of jasmine, her fine-boned face looking so startled and golden and glorious; her glistening, wet lips and body tempting him as she'd towel-dried her glossy ringlets.

She'd had every right to be there as she'd aptly pointed out.

At the sight of those sparkling droplets of water clinging to the grapelike tips of her dusky nipples, his groin had hardened. His blood had coursed like lava.

He'd felt like a beast. Even now he wanted to rush her, to jam her against the wall and take her then and there. He wanted to taste those lips again, to lick those nipples, to lick other secret places until she moaned in ecstasy, to run his hands through her thick, springy curls. Yes, he'd wanted to drown himself in Cici Bellefleur.

How could he still want her with every cell in his being, despite their past? Why did he keep remembering how her golden curls had spread across his pillow like a Southern belle's fan every night after they'd made love? Or how he'd liked to trace her soft, swollen lips with his fingertip, regretting more with every night that passed that his obsession for her had grown with every kiss, with every touch until he'd wanted her for himself far more than Jake had ever wanted her. Then he'd begun to agonize about how painful it would be to give up something so beautiful and infinitely precious to him.

But Grandpère's view had been that Cici was just like his mother—a poor girl out to better herself at their expense—that she would lead him around by the nose as his mother had led his father, that she would spend every last cent of their money until they were completely ruined.

Grandpère kept repeating that he'd had to be tough on him because he'd been too soft on his father and Jake. And as a result of his earlier failure to be firm, the family business was on the verge of bankruptcy, and Jake was wild and out of control. Everything, his grandfather warned, depended upon Logan making a prudent marriage and then settling down to save Claiborne Energy.

Grandpère's opinion about Logan's parents' marriage and the decline in the family fortune had been too true. Their once-proud family and company were on the brink of ruin. Sacrifices had to be made, his grandfather had said, and there was no one else to make them except Logan.

"Don't disappoint me, too, the way your father and brother have always disappointed me," his grandfather said when Logan had been reluctant to come between Jake and Cici. The next night Logan had seduced her to save his brother, and Jake had caught them in bed together. Jake had quit the family in disgust without ever knowing why Logan had acted as he had or that Logan had been cruelly caught in his own trap.

Maybe initially Logan had obeyed his grandfather and slept with Cici to save his brother and his family from ruin, but no sooner had he started making love to her than other forces had him taken over and he'd realized he'd always wanted her for himself.

Still, he soon knew he had to break up with Cici, too, that she was no better as a mate for him than she'd been for Jake. He hadn't wanted to hurt her by caring for her and making her care. He'd hoped that in time he'd forget her and that she'd forget him, too.

When he'd married Noelle, he'd told himself the man who'd loved Cici was dead. But today all the longings of that younger self had clamored inside the man he was now. She was more appealing to him than ever.

Why had Cici saved the picture of him that had been

taken at one of the lowest moments in his life, the day of Noelle's funeral, when he'd come to terms with what a bastard he'd been, and not just to Cici?

He'd been devastated at Noelle's death, but for all the wrong reasons. He'd known then he'd never loved her. That he'd only ever wanted her half as much as he'd always wanted Cici, and he hated himself for that.

Nine years ago he'd believed he'd done the right thing in jilting Cici and marrying Noelle. But his marriage to Noelle was what hadn't worked. Nothing in his personal life had succeeded since Cici.

Deliberately Logan forced his big hand to loosen its crushing grip on his second tall glass of iced tea with a sprig of mint and a slice of lemon. If only the heat in his blood for Cici would lessen.

Alicia would be waiting for him tonight in New Orleans. A sane, mature man would stop lusting after Cici's lush, naked body. But he wasn't sane. And the memory of how she'd looked wetly aglow and achingly vulnerable in the rosy sunlight wouldn't quit.

Maybe Cici's grammar was better—she was a damned good writer, if an annoying one—but was she any more suited to him now than she had been then? She'd always been antiestablishment; a rebel, and an adventuress, while he was conservative to the core. Hell, her uncle was very little short of being an outlaw.

Did those differences really matter in the twenty-first century? Or did the raw, true, primal desire he felt for Cici matter more?

No. He'd been carefully taught that money and breeding and power and the willingness to accept responsibilities that came with position separated people like him from her. He made rules and followed them; she and her uncle stomped over every rule in the book. Nothing was sacred to her. Not even death. Her books and photos proved that.

For money she'd taken a picture of a child being stalked by vultures to horrify her audience of human vultures avid for such shots of lurid misery. At odd moments the picture still haunted him. How could he feel any sympathy for a woman who had lived off the suffering of others?

His feelings for her were driven solely by lust. He'd been obsessed by her in the past. He wasn't about to let his animal urges take over and ruin his life or hers again.

But, oh, God, why did she have to be as lovely as ever—hell, maybe even lovelier? Why did one glimpse of her make his heart open wide and throb with regret? Make him feel as if crucial years of their lives had been cruelly stolen from them?

He was wondering what the cure for such a severe case of lust was—a speedy marriage to the refined Alicia or taking Cici one more time to get her out of his system?—when the front door opened and his grandfather came out holding onto Noonoon's arm.

At the sight of his much stronger and more vigorous grandfather, he did a double take. Gone was the frail, ghostly shadow who had lain in his bed in Baton Rouge

less than a month ago and had weepily confided in
Logan that he wished he was dead. That's when Logan
had left no stone unturned to find the perfect situation
in New Orleans for his ailing grandfather.

Logan slugged his iced tea and set his glass down and
shot to his feet eagerly. "Grandpère! Where's your
walker?"

"Kept tripping over the damn nuisance," Pierre said,
sounding gruff, almost angry, almost his old authorita-
tive self. "Cici got me this quad cane." He let go of
Noonoon and shook it.

Cici. Glad as Logan was that his grandfather was so
much better, he resented that her name alone was
enough to make him flush with heat. Would Noonoon
and Grandpère see and understand?

The old man lifted his cane in a commanding
fashion. "Cici suggested I use a wheelchair when we
give our afternoon tour, though. Don't like to, 'cause
it makes me look old."

Our tour.

"You're nearly eighty."

"Cici says age is just an attitude."

"She should have seen you in the hospital."

"I'm glad she didn't!"

"Okay. Look, I don't want to quarrel or remind you
of unhappier times." Logan went to him, and they
embraced fondly. "I'm glad you're better," he said. "You
feel solid…so much stronger…heavier."

"He's had the appetite of a horse ever since Cici

started cooking him gumbo and making his favorite spicy boudin with red beans for him. Cici does love to cook. She always did!"

The old man's blue eyes flashed at her name, and a tinge of brilliant color dotted his plumper cheeks. "Cici's been great. She's given me a whole new lease on life. I'm almost glad I had the damn stroke. Don't think she'd be fussin' over me if I hadn't."

The sparkle in his eyes and the intensity of his smile made him look ten years younger. "By the way, did you get our invitation?"

"*Our* invitation?"

"For my eightieth birthday party next Saturday. You didn't R.S.V.P. Cici thought you'd probably be too busy to come. Well, are you?" His grandfather's eyes reproached him.

"I didn't receive any invitation, so I didn't know anything about it. And I don't have my calendar," Logan replied, his voice even.

"Your invitation must have gotten lost in the mail," Cici said with false gaiety behind him.

Lost, my ass. The sexy witch had no doubt cleverly excluded him.

Logan whirled and felt another rush of unwelcome heat as they locked eyes for the length of several, thudding heartbeats. Unable to resist dragging his gaze lower, he noted a pink T-shirt stretching across her ample breasts that read T-Bos's Bar under a stenciled biker's face. Her skintight jeans had holes in the knees.

T-Bos's was a successful biker bar of unsavory reputation that her uncle Bos defied the Claibornes by running on his property next door to Belle Rose.

There should be a law against shirts like that, at least on bodies like hers. The jersey knit hugged her breasts and waist even more snugly than her jeans cupped her ass. Not that he was surprised at her getup. It was sexy as hell, just like the woman who wore it. Conservative, she wasn't.

"Jake is coming," she taunted softly. Or did he only imagine the challenge in her husky voice?

"You invited Jake? And not me?"

"Still competitive?"

"Damn it, no!" His feelings for his alienated twin were more complicated than that single word could possibly describe. "How could I be? Because of you, I haven't talked to him in nine years."

"Only…because of *me?* How easily we forget."

"I've called him, but he refuses my calls," Logan said.

"Do you really blame him?"

Her question reminded him of all he'd done to come between Jake and her once again.

"I'm sorry." She paused. "I don't want to quarrel. I hadn't talked to him either until a few weeks ago. He's been living in Orlando, although I expect you know that…just like I expect you know that he set up a branch of his business in New Orleans after Katrina."

He knew. Jake, a successful architect and builder in Florida, had pledged his support to help rebuild New Orleans after two major hurricanes had nearly destroyed it. Not that Jake ever bothered to look him up when he'd breezed into the city to check his operations. And he didn't blame him.

"I thought it was a shame we'd never talked since that last summer," she said, "so one day I just picked up the phone and called him."

"And he answered?"

She nodded. "Why wouldn't he? I guess my name showed up on his Caller ID. He had no reason to be mad at me. We must have talked for at least half an hour."

"About what?"

"If you come to the party, you can ask him yourself."

"Again, I'll have to check my calendar."

"You will come, won't you?" Grandpère said, his voice weaker, maybe because he'd been up too long.

At his grandfather's question, Logan felt trapped. *Damn.*

"He had so much fun planning his party, and Cici's worked so hard on it," Noonoon pleaded softly. "I'll go inside and get you an invitation."

"A hundred people have already accepted," Cici added. "Lots of them are your friends. I let them think the party was your idea."

"Me? Why how generous of you."

The three of them were all staring at him, waiting, their eyes begging him to say he'd attend. Funny how he could go for the jugular in business, and in a family situation that involved upsetting Grandpère, he was ready to cave in an instant.

"All right. All right. I know when I'm beaten. I'll give the party top priority." After a pause, he continued. "Cici, I need to get back to New Orleans. Tonight. I have a date."

"With Alicia Butler?" Cici's eyebrows arched. "Of Butler Shipyards?"

"And just how in the hell do you know that?" He stopped himself, when he saw her smile.

"I'm a journalist. I read the gossip columns."

He ignored her answer. "You and I need to discuss your lease. Did you bring it with you?"

"Sorry." Cici, who cupped her hands over her mouth, didn't look the least bit sorry. "Forgot."

Like hell.

A woman sharp enough to know what was going on in his personal life better than he did had deliberately refused to bring it just to provoke him.

"Well, go get it!" he thundered.

"All right," Cici purred, smiling at an alarmed Noonoon and Pierre. But just as she turned to go, her gaze darted toward the back of the house and then to her watch. "Oh, dear…. Bad timing. Looks like our tour has assembled. "Noonoon," she said. "I know this is a lot to ask, with all you have to do, but if you wouldn't mind wheeling Pierre around back—you and he could start our last tour of the day. You won't have to say anything…if you'd just be kind enough to push him. I'd do it, but Mr. Claiborne insists he wants to discuss my lease. Maybe by the time the tour is over, he and I will be finished with each other, and he can be on his way."

Cici's sweet smile made Logan wish he had a nail or two to chew. "After all he has a very important date with Alicia Butler. Butler Shipyards."

Feeling like he was about to explode again, Logan nodded curtly toward Noonoon. When Noonoon walked over to Pierre, Cici ran back to the *garçonnière* to fetch the document she should have brought with her in the first place. Fuming, he watched her retreating bottom in those skintight jeans with way too much interest.

Not for the first time today, he told himself to calm down, reminding himself that he was firmly in control, that when she returned, he would be so utterly ruthless she would soon be packing her bags.

"I said I'll double the money you paid my naive grandfather, if you'll be so kind as to rip up this worthless piece of garbage and leave tomorrow morning."

Logan relaxed a little when Cici, who was sitting on a wide wicker chair on the gallery, was quiet, her brow furrowed as if she were considering his most generous offer. Then she looked up from the document and smiled at him, blushing so prettily he itched to caress her.

When her sparkling eyes teased, luring him, he should have been warned.

"If I sleep with you, for old times' sake, would you let me stay?" Her voice was soft and husky, shaking a little, yet her invitation flowed through him like music, causing something vital and true, something ripe and raw, in him to leap toward her.

"What?" he growled, his gaze lowering to her breasts despite his best intentions, because he was truly tempted by her outrageous offer. Which she, no doubt, knew.

Damn her silky hide.

She laughed at him. "Oh, dear, even your ears are turning red. Why is that, I wonder?"

Because he felt as hot as a volcano about to burst.

"Quit staring at my breasts like I'm offering them to you on a serving platter! I was just kidding. Okay? You looked so grim and uptight I thought a little levity would do us both good."

"Well, I wouldn't kid about something like that, if I were you," he snapped.

"Why? Because you're mad that you want to sleep with me too much?"

"I don't want to sleep with you." His voice sounded strange to his ears, maybe because he was speaking through gritted teeth.

"Good," she said in a teasing tone that said she didn't believe a single word. "Because I don't want you, either. So, we're both safe. In no sexual danger from each other. You have your pretty Alicia, aka Butler Shipyards, and I have my work in progress."

"No boyfriend?"

Why in hell had he asked that? He didn't give a damn whether she had a boyfriend or not.

"Would you care?"

"Stop it."

"I can ask a question if I want. You don't have the right to tell me what to say or do any more."

"I never told you any such thing. We weren't ever that important to each other."

"Thanks. They say it's good for one's character to be humbled once in a while."

"I want you off my land. If you don't agree to my terms, I'll have my lawyer contact you. Trust me. The fight over the legality of this lease will cost you far more than it's worth. If you're smart, you'll take my offer."

"I can tell you've grown used to pushing people around."

"Damn it."

"You know, I almost feel sorry for you. Nine years haven't taught you anything. Oh, sure, you're richer and colder, which means a lot of people probably think you're pretty successful. But I'll bet you're not nearly as happy and as satisfied with your life as you try to pretend, or you wouldn't be trying to bully me. You're living a lie, Logan Claiborne, and I'm one of the few people who knows it. That's why you want me to leave. You don't want to face the truth about who you really are and what you really feel. You're no elegant, refined gentleman. You use your money like a shield to fend off anything that's real…like me."

"Rip up that paper. Do the smart thing for once. Just say you'll take my money."

"Or you'll what?" When she licked her mouth, making her lower lip shine wetly, something that had been wound too tight for nine damn years snapped inside him, unleashing a force he would have denied with every breath in his body.

With a suddenness that startled them both, him most of all, he seized her slim shoulders. Jerking her to her feet, his hard arms circled hers, and then crushed her against him. "You shouldn't have come back here. You shouldn't have messed with me again."

"So, you do want me, a little," she whispered, her musical voice a husky taunt against his throat. "Is that why you're so afraid of me?"

"I'm not afraid. You have to go," he muttered furiously, too aware of her soft breasts mashed against his chest. "You know it. And I know it."

"Do I?" She paused. "Well, now I'm going to tell you something. I don't know it. You and I haven't been on the same page in ever so long, Mr. Claiborne. Lucky me."

"Damn you."

"I want to stay and I will—until I'm good and ready to go. And I will go, but only when I decide."

"If you're smart…"

"I'll what? I'll leave before I tempt you into my bed again?" She laughed.

A faint breeze swept the wide veranda, stirring gold tendrils against her temple. She was so damn sexy, and her body felt so warm, he lost his train of thought. How could he think with her in his arms? With her voluptuous breasts pressed against his chest? With her hair smelling sweetly of shampoo and her body of jasmine scented soap? With her half-open lips too close to his to resist? With her saying things to deliberately tempt him?

Yes, she was right. He wanted her naked and writhing and wet underneath him again.

On that thought his mouth came down on hers. If only she hadn't clung, maybe sanity would have returned. But she did, pressing herself against him, shuddering as violently as he did, causing him to gasp and kiss her again and then again. And with every kiss, his long-repressed hunger grew until it was a thunderous, pulsing fever. When she purred, melted and opened her delicious mouth wider so that his tongue could fill it, the world began to reel past him in a dizzying rush.

He had no idea how long he held her and devoured her mouth, or how he summoned the strength to finally push her away before it was too late to stop.

Panting hard, he stared down at her. He'd been seconds away from carrying her to the *garçonnière* where he would have taken her wildly and violently, not tenderly as he had on their first night. And once would never be enough. He felt as obsessed by her now as he had in the past.

As his guilty eyes held hers, he saw that she was burning up just like he was. Her cheeks were red, her mouth swollen, her eyes aflame, her tumult more than equal to his.

"I still hate you," she said, breathing so hard and fast, those beautiful breasts of hers were heaving, tempting him to new indiscretions.

"I hate you even more than Jake does. I hate you for

what you did in the past. For who you were back then. But most of all, I hate you for who you still are. And for what you just did. You take, but you don't give."

Then why was she running her tongue over her lips as if to taste him again?

"Good," he whispered, loathing himself even more than she and Jake ever could. "Concentrate on that, then, and maybe we'll get through this without tearing up our lives again."

"And I thought I was the only one who suffered," she whispered. "Was I wrong?"

Never in a thousand years would he admit that he'd suffered because of losing her, that he'd caused Noelle to suffer, and yet… The truth was that after he'd jilted Cici and had willed his overpowering attraction for her to die, so that he could marry Noelle and make her happy, his determination had failed him. Back then he'd thought if a man had enough willpower, he could make himself do anything. He'd believed he could create the life of his grandfather's dreams through sheer force of will. But instead his obsession with her had dominated him.

Through the years, she'd haunted him. Every time he'd come home to Belle Rose, even with Noelle, Cici had been there, memories of her sensuality and sweetness luring him.

Why wouldn't her power over him die?

Not daring to look at her a second longer for fear of losing the last fragile shreds of his control, Logan turned and vaulted down the stairs beside the ugly ramp she'd

built. Striding around the back of the house as if ten
demons were on his trail, he called to his grandfather.

Cici came running, her dark eyes wide, as a smiling
Pierre held up a hand to stop the tour, so he could see
what his grandson wanted.

"Is everything all right, Logan?" Pierre asked.

"It's time I left." He took his grandfather's hand and
shook it gently, noting how weak the old man's clasp was.

"Then you're through with Cici and she's free to
finish the tour with me?"

"Yes," Logan muttered. "I'm through with her."

"Wonderful. I'll be happy to finish the tour," Cici
said, her lilting velvety voice so cheery behind him he
was further infuriated although he continued to smile at
his grandfather. No doubt she thought she'd won.

Not that he so much as glanced at Cici as she rushed
up to join his grandfather. Logan didn't meet the gazes
of any of the people clustered around his grandfather
and Cici, either, but he could tell that they sensed some
of the dramatic undercurrents because they were staring
from him to Cici much too avidly.

He did manage to nod a final goodbye to his smiling
grandfather even as he swore to himself that tomorrow
morning, he'd tell Hayes Daniels, his CEO, to sic the
full force of their legal department on the defiant Cici.
The house, after all, which was open to the public,
belonged to Claiborne Energy.

Logan smiled grimly. She wouldn't last long after
such an assault. He would soon be rid of her.

Four

Logan, who had the headache from hell after a night of no sleep, had arrived at his office shortly after 6:00 a.m. Work on the last few details of the merger went smoothly for a couple of hours.

The first sign that Cici had launched a counter attack of her own before he'd even gotten his planes in the air occurred shortly before 9:00 a.m. Logan was just settling into a meeting with Hayes Daniels in Hayes's lavish office after a lengthy chat with their attorneys about Miss Bellefleur, her illegal lease of property on company land and a strategy to deal with her when his secretary called him.

"But this isn't just a phone call," Mrs. Dillings said,

her voice sharp with indignation after he'd dared to point out that he'd given her strict instructions that she was not supposed to interrupt him. "I thought you would want to know that your grandfather's here. Especially since you went down to check on him yesterday."

"Here? In New Orleans?"

"Here. In your office. And if I may say so, he hardly looks like the invalid you described. You'd never know he had a stroke except for that slight limp. But he does seem most anxious to talk to you. He said *immediately*. Oh, and you know how his jaw juts out the way yours does and how you both growl when you're not getting your way? Well…looks like a storm is brewing."

She would know. His grandfather had been her former boss. Obviously, Mrs. Dillings was very good at what she did and knew her value, or she would never have dared to comment like that. Maybe someday Logan should remind her that more people got fired for poor people skills than for being bad at their jobs.

"I'll be right there. See if he wants anything…a cup of coffee…a beignet…hell, order him a dozen beignets."

"He's with a most charming companion. A Miss Bellefleur."

At the mention of Cici's name, a pair of pert breasts stretching a hot pink, jersey top with a biker's nasty face on it arose in his mind's eye, causing his headache to worsen. The same restlessness that had hammered in Logan's blood all night long and had kept him awake began to pulse anew. He arose from his leather chair, walked stiffly to the door and then, stopping himself, began to pace.

"Miss Bellefleur's already asked for a whole tray of beignets. She likes them with extra powdered sugar."

Would she eat all that sugar with a spoon and then lick her fingertips?

He stared out the window at the city which was shrouded in murky mists. Unbidden came the memory of an eighteen-year-old Cici sitting across the table from him under the famous green-and-white canopy of the Café du Monde, licking powdered sugar off the curve of her thumb. How enchanted he'd been by everything she'd done that afternoon.

"Right. Indeed." Heat suffusing him, Logan said a stern goodbye to Mrs. Dillings. Continuing to pace, he directed his attention to Hayes, who was leaning back in his black leather chair, his long, muscular legs crossed, his tanned fingertips steepled in front of him.

"She's here," Logan said.

"Who?" Hayes said smiling, his black eyes mild as he studied him.

"Cici," Logan snapped as if such a question were ridiculous.

"Our infamous Miss Bellefleur." Hayes leaned forward. His black eyes became piercing, which was bothersome.

"Well, that didn't take our lawyers long. We barely hung up and now the villain's here to plead her case," Hayes said, his smile broadening.

"Obviously our attorneys failed to reach her. Because she's here and not at Belle Rose, where she belongs, so she could have answered the damn phone."

"I thought the point was that she *doesn't* belong there."

"Right. Exactly. Of course. *But my point now is that she jumped the gun. Again.*"

"Your Cici is beginning to sound like a handful."

Of course, any woman foolhardy enough to risk her neck in war zones, the long lens of her Leica camera her only shield against bullets, is bound to be a handful.

"She's not *my* Cici!" he yelled, he who never yelled.

"If you say so. All you've talked about is her. Nothing—ever—not even your wife has ever distracted you like this."

"Because she's using my grandfather to get to me."

"Dirty trick."

"She's full of them."

Hayes, his best friend, his former college roommate, his CEO, was tall and dark and tough as nails, way tougher than Logan. Which was why Logan had hired him. The trouble was, Hayes, who was nosy as hell, was observing him with far too much interest and probably far too much insight.

"I'd better go deal with her," Logan said.

"But you just brought in our legal team so you wouldn't have to be involved with her personally. Why not send Abe? You said you didn't want to get your hands dirty. You said this is a trivial, domestic matter."

"Right. That's what I said."

Suddenly, this whole matter with Cici felt way too personal to turn over to anybody else, even his ruthless lawyers, of which Abe was the head.

"Did I ever tell you how much I dislike being slammed with my own data?"

Hayes laughed out loud. "Don't we all? Keep me posted. I want to hear how round two comes out. Your Cici is much more interesting than any merger with Butler Shipyards. By the way, I'm beginning to wonder if Mitchell Butler has been entirely honest with us. At this point it's just a gut feeling…but…"

"Check it out," Logan said.

Logan's heart had been beating at a ferocious clip ever since he'd shut his door only to see Cici and his grandfather, their chairs pushed close together, enjoying a makeshift picnic of beignets and rich black coffee. Oblivious to the crumbs they'd scattered all over his coffee table, they were smiling at each other.

The old man looked happier than he had in years, and that would have been heartwarming if Logan trusted Cici. But how would his grandfather feel when Cici finished her book and returned to putting her life on the line in the fast lane just to take a few pictures? Cici was an adventuress, not a caregiver.

Sitting down at his desk, Logan punched a button on his intercom and told Mrs. Dillings to hold his calls. When he looked up his grandfather had moved his chair so that it faced Logan's desk.

When the old man frowned, Logan scrunched lower in his chair. Nobody could make Logan feel four years old again just by sticking out his jaw except this man who'd raised him. How many times had he stood in this very same office when it had belonged to his grandfather and waited for the old man to begin some lecture because he'd committed some minor, boyish infraction?

As he waited, Logan began to feel caged in his civilized office that was filled with leather and chrome and too many polished wooden surfaces. And he knew who to blame for his discomfiture.

Not that he was about to give the delectable Miss Bellefleur, who was, indeed, licking her fingertips with a grace any feline would envy, the satisfaction of looking at her.

Even so, all he saw was Cici. All he felt was her.

In her purple T-shirt and tight black jeans, with her childishly sticky fingers, fingers he wanted to lick clean, she was a garish splash of voluptuous color in his too elegant, beige suite.

Did she always have to dress in outfits that screamed, *look at me?* Did she even own a decent dress? Or a conservative suit? Or plain black pumps that might have concealed those livid, purple toenails, which, by the way, on *her,* were sexy as hell? At least, they matched her T-shirt.

He had memories about those half-naked feet. After sex, she used to climb on top of him and stretch out, placing the soles of her feet on top of his feet. God, he'd loved the feel of her on top of him as he'd wondered what she'd do next.

And her hair—it was wild this morning—springy curls tumbling to her shoulders. Big hair was not a look he liked on his woman…usually…except right after sex. Still, he was hard as a rock, and the view wasn't what was turning him on.

Ignoring Cici, Logan concentrated on his grandfather. "You seem upset, Grandpère. Why are you here?"

"Maybe because sitting around Belle Rose isn't doing me much good. I was always a man of action."

"Yes, you were."

"I'm here because I want to start by righting a few wrongs."

"Such as?"

"In the past, I was unfair to Cici. And so were you."

"At whose instigation?" Logan whispered.

"Mine. I take full responsibility. I was so furious at Bos and so discouraged by your father's failures and Jake's wildness, I didn't want Jake to be seduced by Cici and marry her. I didn't know what a niece of Bos's might do to our property if she married into our family. I didn't trust her. So, I asked you to intervene to save your brother, who was always more susceptible to temptation than you."

Little did he know.

"And because I did, Cici was hurt so badly she ran away and got into a dangerous, heartbreaking profession. She stayed away, until now."

"Is that what she told you?"

He nodded. "Last night we had a long talk."

Logan could well imagine that they had.

"She wants to come home," Pierre said. "She says she forgives me. She's persuaded Jake to come home, which is what I've wanted ever since I got sick. And for that, now you want to throw her out."

After such noble praise of Cici, Logan's gaze swung across the room to the young woman. Her fragile face framed by masses of gold curls looked tense and shadowed in the morning light. Beneath his scrutiny, she blushed and averted her eyes.

"Last I heard, Belle Rose isn't and never was her home," Logan said. "She should lease some other place. Grandpère, I don't think…she's the best influence on you…in your present state."

"Let me be the judge of that. I'm not the man I was, and Cici's never been the girl I thought she was."

Logan swallowed. He felt guiltier than he ever had for the past, so it didn't help when he noticed Cici's hands that were knotted in her lap were trembling.

Had she had trouble sleeping last night, too. Had she relived that damn kiss on the gallery again and again as he had, wanting more? Or did she hate his guts as she had every right to do?

"I want you to relent and let her stay…near me," his grandfather persisted.

For another long moment Logan's gaze lingered on Cici's pale, contrite face. Strangely, he felt touched by his grandfather's request and like his grandfather, ashamed of his own actions nine years ago.

Most of all he hurt. But he couldn't undo the past. Jake had left because he was furious at Logan for doing his grandfather's bidding by bedding Cici just so he couldn't have her. He'd said he was tired of the way the Claibornes always thought they could manipulate other peoples' lives.

Logan had tried to explain why he'd acted as he had to Jake at the time. "Grandpère said the family couldn't afford another marriage like our parents'. One of us had to do the smart thing. He knew you'd probably go the whole nine yards, including marriage if you slept with her, so he told me to make love to her. To save you, Jake," he'd said.

"What are you, his puppet? Cici doesn't deserve that. She's not like Mother. You're not like Daddy. Funny, I used to think that was a good thing. I used to admire you. You always worked so hard, made such good grades. Now, I just want out of this family."

Jake's fist had slammed into Logan's jaw on his way out. Logan hadn't seen him since.

Suddenly the wrenching pain of the past held Logan's heart in a death grip. He'd thrown Cici away, blindly, stupidly. He'd told himself he'd done it for Jake. For his grandfather. For the family. And for Cici even, because she would have been unhappy in his uptight conservative world. He'd convinced himself he'd done the right thing.

Damn it, he'd been so sure of himself back then.

But could he say he'd acted honorably toward all concerned? Toward Cici?

Logan shut his eyes. Then he pressed his eyelids and sucked in a long breath.

"I've always trusted you to do the right thing," his grandfather said. "You used to watch out for your brother. It was almost like you were older and wiser. Because I trusted you, when Jake ran out, I cut him off without a cent, and I gave you the reins of Claiborne Energy. And, yes, you made the family a fortune. I was proud of you, boy. Back then that was all I cared about."

"And now…"

"For nine years I've been estranged from Jake, and now Cici tells me he's doing well. She says that after he ran off, he went back to school, that he's done wonderful things in Florida and in New Orleans."

"I tried to tell you…"

"Before I got sick, I was a stubborn fool. I didn't want to hear about him, did I? Praise of him made me feel guilty. I know I tried to teach you to be exactly like me, but I was wrong about that, too. Don't be like me, boy. If I've learned anything in this last month when I've felt so weak and old and useless, it's that a grandson like Jake is worth more than any amount of money. I should never have set you on a collision course with your twin and then disinherited him for getting angry at us. And now…for Cici's help in talking Jake into coming to my birthday party, I want to repay her kindness by letting her live in the *garçonnière*."

"Did you ever think that maybe the reason Jake's such a success now is because I saved him from Cici? From the way she's been playing you since her return, I'm beginning to think you had her figured right back then."

Uttering a soft, wounded cry, Cici sprang to her feet. In a halting voice she whispered, "I can't listen to this. I'll be right outside, Pierre. Don't wear yourself out defending me." Then on a whisper of wood trailing across carpet, the door closed behind her.

"It's my fault you think she's as trashy as Bos. But you're wrong. She's a very sensitive woman with a great heart, and she's made a success of her career…even if it hasn't been all that lucrative. I want to help her, to make up just a little for what I did in the past."

Had she been whining about money to his grandfather at a time when he'd been weak and needy? Was that what she wanted—money?

"Did it ever occur to you that maybe she's using you to get back at me? For sleeping with her? For jilting her?"

"Cici would never do that."

"Oh, wouldn't she?"

Abe stalked into the office before Logan, who wondered if he wasn't being set up, could say no more.

"If this is a bad moment…" Abe paused.

Pierre cleared his throat. "No. It's a wonderful moment."

After a few more seconds of silence so tense it nearly

hummed, the old man continued. "I'm glad you got here this fast, Abe. Things around here are about to change. I'm tired of rest and relaxation at home. It's time we moved forward. First, I'll be coming into the office twice a week—starting Monday. Second, I'll be moving into my old office. The young lady who's waiting for me outside has hired me a driver."

"Grandpère, do you really think you're strong enough? It's bad enough that Cici is using you to get back at me."

"Third," his stubborn grandfather continued with a frown, "I'll want you to write up an airtight lease. On the *garçonnière* behind Belle Rose for the little lady in the waiting room. Miss Bellefleur is a long-time family friend. Really, she's practically a granddaughter. She'll be wanting a twelve-month lease."

"Twelve months? You can't be serious, Grandpère."

Again his grandfather ignored him.

"You see, Abe, she's writing a book with the working title, *Lords of the Bayou.*"

Logan stared gloomily at his polished desk. No doubt she'd slam him as the environmentalist's worst nightmare. He'd have all the tree huggers picketing him again.

"The *garçonnière* is quiet," Pierre continued. "She says the setting is perfect for her research, especially since I'm there to help her. She's won all sorts of awards, so it'll be an honor to have her, not to mention a joy to work with her. I have a library full of history books on the subject, and I can put her in contact with all the right people."

Logan had the power to override his grandfather's decisions, but he loved and respected the old man too much to belittle him like that.

Fortunately, the tense meeting with his grandfather, who began to fade the moment Abe left, didn't last much longer. No sooner had Cici ushered the old man downstairs to her Miata than Hayes walked in, his excuse being a thick stack of legal documents on the Butler merger that needed his signature.

"From the look of your face, I'd say it's pretty clear who won round two. But cheer up. She's damn sure worked a miracle where your grandfather is concerned. The old man looked as fit as a bull when he was climbing into her sports car. Nothing like a young girl to get an old man's blood up, now is there?"

Suddenly, for no reason at all Logan wanted to punch Hayes's lights out.

"Hey, how come you didn't mention she was a knockout?"

"Don't...don't say another word. And as for her being a knockout, if you know what's good for you, you'll stay the hell away from her."

"I see. You sure had me fooled. Me and everybody else. We all thought you were serious about Alicia."

"You don't see a damn thing. I am serious about Alicia!" Logan thundered.

"Right." But Hayes's dark eyes were glinting, and the

corners of his lips were twitching with amusement, as he fought a losing battle not to smile.

"You said Mitchell Butler's story might have a few holes in it."

"So far it's only a hunch."

A sad, lost, homesick feeling swamped Cici as something vicious stung her above the elbow.

"Ouch!"

She quit knocking on her uncle's door long enough to slap at two giant mosquitoes on her arm.

Closing her eyes, she listened for a long moment. Not that she could hear anything from inside her uncle's cabin over the chorus of whistles and chirps coming from the swamp.

"Uncle Bos, why don't you open the door? I know you're in there. I know you left the bar because I've already been there and Tommy told me you're not feeling well. He sent me over with some of his spicy boudin, made just the way you like it. And Noonoon and I cooked up a big pot of gator gumbo. The roux came out real good. We threw in some cayenne pepper, onion, celery and bell pepper.

She drew a breath and stared at the huge stack of wire crawfish traps, gill nets and hoop nets leaning against the ten-foot pilings beneath her uncle's shack. "Uncle Bos, I'm beginning to feel stupid yelling at your door."

Her gaze wandered from the bayou with its dark, funereal vegetation, past the wreckage of his old rooster pens, to the ruined ponds behind their sagging fences where she used to help him raise thousands of little turtles that they'd marketed as pets to kids all over America. Other than the aluminum outboard tied at the end of his dock near the thick stand of tall rozo cane instead of her red pirogue, not much had changed.

Well, maybe the dark brown water had crept a little closer to the house, land being a vanishing commodity in Louisiana thanks to Logan and his kind.

"Okay. If you're going to be stubborn, I'll just leave the pots on your doorstep and come back for 'em later. When you're done, you can leave 'em outside for me to pick up."

Slowly she climbed down his stairs and walked past his motorcycle and then further out onto the dock to stare at the glimmering reflections in the bayou. Sagging posted No Trespassing signs were nailed to every cypress tree trunk. Her uncle, who'd always been something of a loner, wasn't the most welcoming type.

No wonder she'd never felt like she belonged. Uncle Bos certainly hadn't wanted her. She'd been eight when her parents had been washed away by a wall of water caused by a crevasse, or a break in a levee, when the Mississippi had run too high one spring. Luckily she'd clung to a board that had swept her to a tree where she'd held on to a branch for hours.

No, her uncle hadn't wanted to take in an orphaned niece, but he'd been her only relative. And he hadn't believed in public welfare. At least, not for any relative of his, even if she'd been a little sissy who didn't know the first thing about life in the wilderness.

He hadn't understood her reading or her fascination with pictures in magazines. He'd called her lazy for writing and extravagant for shooting so much film. He'd quit school after the sixth grade because in his view education was a waste of time. Real life was fishing and trapping and hunting and carving and drinking, and pitting one of his prized cocks against another's and laying bets. He'd made a small fortune cockfighting before it had been outlawed. Not that he was always a man to follow the law.

She and he had had nearly nothing, other than their mutual love of the swamp in common. Yes, she'd come to love the swamp, so mostly she'd tried to stay out of his way. Then, to make matters worse, there'd been the times when he'd vanished for days on end, maybe to attend illegal cockfights. Maybe to drink in the houseboat he kept in the swamp. Maybe to be with a woman. Who knew?

She'd hated being alone, but she hadn't told anybody because she'd been too afraid the authorities would take her away from him. Logan may have suspected her plight because often when her uncle disappeared, he'd sent Noonoon over or had come himself to check on her and bring her food.

Back then, before Uncle Bos had fallen out with the Claibornes over his bar and cockfights, he'd worked part-time as a gardener at Belle Rose. She'd loved going over to the plantation, loved following the Claiborne twins around, loved hearing about all the exciting things they were doing from Noonoon, who'd often let her inside to help in the kitchen.

Everything at Belle Rose had seemed beautiful and as magical as the places she'd read about in books. After the twins' parents' fatal car wreck, Pierre had welcomed them. He hadn't disappeared for weeks without telling them where he'd gone. He hadn't made them feel lost and left out or like they didn't belong. He'd taken them on wonderful vacations, too. When they returned, she'd pestered them into telling her everything they'd seen and done and into showing her their pictures.

How she'd longed for the stability she'd known with her parents, but that was a vanished world, one she only dimly remembered. Once her uncle had taken her to her old neighborhood. A new house had stood where her family's home had been. The place had seemed empty and utterly foreign to her. She'd felt alienated. It was as if she'd never lived there. As if her life with her parents had been completely erased. How she'd craved to feel some sense of belonging somewhere.

Over time Belle Rose had become a symbol for the kind of home and loving family life and stability she'd longed for but didn't think anyone like her could ever achieve again.

Cici leaned over and stared into the dark water. When she caught sight of her own reflection, she laughed out loud. Talk about a bad hair day!

Driving over to her uncle's with the top down hadn't

done her crazy, Princess Leia hairdo any good. She looked like she'd sprouted a pair of wild pompoms above each ear. With a smile she remembered watching part of an old Star Wars movie with Noonoon's grand-daughter, who'd wanted to pretend she was Princess Leia after the film was over. Cici had fixed Latasha's hair and then her own.

She was still laughing at the memory when she heard the unmistakable sound of a big car on the gravel road. Turning, her smile dissolved the second she recognized the grim, broad-shouldered man in the silver Lexus pulling up beside her Miata.

What was *he* doing here? Logan Claiborne was the last person she felt like talking to after the horribly humiliating scene in his office yesterday. He wasn't welcome here, either. Her uncle held a long-standing grudge against all Claibornes.

Squaring her shoulders she headed toward the tall man in the three-piece black suit who was swinging himself out of his car while scowling at her.

Ignoring the acceleration of her heart and his forbidding expression, she said, "Didn't you see the signs? You're not exactly welcome here, you know. Tommy told me…"

Logan shot her a tight smile. "Tommy can go straight to hell." As always his narrowed, blue gaze lingered a little too long on her breasts.

She was wearing a tight black T-shirt today with big pink letters that said, *Pretty Woman*. Not that the T-shirt was anything a Princess Leia clone should be caught dead wearing.

"You're not too welcome here yourself from what I hear," he said.

"Your being here will make me even less popular, but that's none of your business. I've been reading up on the Butler-Claiborne merger on the Web. Don't you have big important rich guy stuff to be doing back in New Orleans? Or maybe you could drill up more of the wilderness we both used to love, digging your canals to get to your well heads and thus destroying the natural water flow, your machines throwing so much mud up on the banks, you smother all the vegetation and habitat for good."

His eyes climbed from her breasts up her throat to her face with such searing intensity she blushed. When he suddenly smiled, she wondered if it had anything to do with her crazy hairdo.

"Cici, why did you come home? What do you want? Why are you hanging out with my grandfather and pestering me?"

"I could argue as to who's pestering who. This is my home, too, you know."

"Is it? Did your uncle ever really want you?"

She took a deep, painful breath. "That tack won't win you any points. And as for Pierre, I like him. Ours is a friendship born of mutual need."

"I thought you ran away to get away from all this. This place must seem pretty tame to a woman who's lived like you have."

"No, I ran away from you. From how you made me feel, which was cheap and horrible, if that gives you any satisfaction. Talk about jumping from the frying pan into the fire. It didn't take me long to discover there are worse monsters than you. And by the way, you don't know anything about how I lived…although I imagine you think I lived wild and loose."

"What'll it take for you to go away again?"

"Maybe it's time you learned that I have as much right to be here as you do."

"Your uncle doesn't want you any more than he ever did. I don't see him opening his damn door. Not even for Noonoon's gumbo."

"He will. He's just being stubborn." Her lips curved. "Like a lot of other people…you," she taunted.

"He and I are nothing alike."

"You say you don't want me. I don't think you mean that any more than he does. I think I'm messing things up for you, maybe…maybe because you don't feel like you pretend—indifferent to me."

Logan's head jerked back as if she'd slapped him. "Shut up," he whispered even as he stepped thrillingly closer.

"Okay. Then why did you kiss me? And why are you looking at my lips like you want to do it again?"

"Stop it."

"No. Because maybe I can't stop what I feel any more than you can."

"I can stop it, all right."

"Right." She laughed. "You're the guy with all the

willpower. You probably skip lunch to jog. So, why'd you leave your fancy office and track me here?"

"I came here to work out a compromise."

"No. You didn't. You want what you want. The problem is maybe so do I. And maybe I've finally learned to go after what I want."

There was a startled cry from the swamp. They both turned as a blue heron flapped its wide, gray wings and took flight, skimming low just above the brown water.

"You know what I think, Logan," she said, turning back to him and finding his eyes glued to her face. "I think we've both caught the same fever. If you're so sure you're immune to me, kiss me again. Prove I'm wrong about you. About *us.*"

"There is no *us.*"

"So, prove it, big guy. Kiss me."

When he took a step backward, probably to seek the safety of his car, she reached out and grabbed his tie. Reeling him close, she stepped into his arms.

Stiffening, he stood up straighter. For a second, she was sure he'd push her away and barricade himself in that tank of a car. But he just stood there on the edge of surrender, his heart pounding so hard she could feel it.

She pulled him even closer. "Kiss me."

In the next instant his breath was hot and ragged against her forehead.

"I don't want to hurt you again," he whispered even as she tightened her hold on his tie. "I'm no good for you."

And with those words, which were better than an

apology somehow, the worst of her anger and hurt that she'd been harboring for so long melted a little.

Gently, she let go of his tie and touched his thick, dark hair, combing her fingers through it, mussing it a little further. Then she reached up and, framing his face with her hands, she placed her lips gently against his throat.

"I've always liked your hair," she said. "It's one thing about you that's always a mess."

He smiled. "You don't know the half of it."

In the next instant his hard mouth was on hers, tasting sweeter than honey and burning hotter than a flame, but then it always had, even if that was a cliché. His mouth sent fire dancing through her veins as she melted against him.

The kiss was unlike the last one because he wasn't fighting it, and neither was she. Their lips joined them. Every part of him belonged to her in that primeval man-woman way that felt wilder and more dangerous than the swamp.

His hungry mouth still locked on hers, he tightened his hold on her, pulling her even closer, his muscular arms binding her to him. Not that she had any desire to run from his kisses or the possession of his powerful embrace. No, like a fool, like before when she'd been a naive kid, she wanted to stay in his arms forever and do all the naughty, forbidden things they'd done before. Was she a fool or what? Yes. Where Logan Claiborne was concerned, the answer was all too obvious.

Unfortunately, Uncle Bos must've been spying on them all along. Suspecting her of having less than wise instincts where Logan Claiborne was concerned, Bos banged his door open and hollered down to her.

"If you come by for a visit with me, girl, I'm up here waitin'. The door's wide open. But it won't be for long unless you get rid of him, yes. If you miss the chance, the next time you see me I might be laying up in my coffin."

"Well," she said, smiling triumphantly up at Logan. "See, he does too want me. And maybe, just maybe I'm right about you wanting me just a little bit, too, yes?"

Logan pulled her against him and held her close so that she was in no doubt about the hardness or size of his erection. "Maybe a little, but just like always, the old cuss's timing's lousy."

With a shaky laugh, she raised her hand and smoothed his sensual lips which were still hot with a gentle fingertip.

"See you," she promised huskily.

"Cici, I don't want to hurt you. This isn't going to work."

Why not, because I come from this hovel on stilts half sunk in rot and muck and you come from your beautiful, charmed Belle Rose? Will I never, ever be good enough?

Not that she spoke such truths aloud. She wasn't in the mood for a quarrel or a reality check. No, she had much more appealing ideas about how to spend her time with Logan Claiborne.

"You really do need to go," he chided. "I never considered your Uncle Bos a patient man."

She smiled, causing him to grin, too. "You have a beautiful mouth," she said. "Lots of straight, white teeth."

"The better to eat you with."

"Naughty boy."

His eyes glinted as they moved over her face and then down her T-shirt. Tipping her chin with a finger-tip, he gently nicked her nose with his teeth. "Naughty girl."

"You do have a point." Fluffing her pompoms, she swished her hips, just to get his mind on her ass where it belonged. Turning, she left him.

Feeling his heated gaze burning into her spine, she put more swing into her hips and really began to strut.

Not once did she look back or say another word, not even a sultry goodbye.

He chuckled out loud.

It was amazing how well they could get along if they stopped talking.

The inside of her uncle's cabin was as dark and musty as ever, maybe mustier. Imagining all sorts of terrible molds, Cici itched to open all the windows and take a scrub brush soaked in chlorine or lemon juice and scour every surface.

"You knocking on Logan Claiborne's doors, too? Bringing him gumbo? Trying to win his heart since he be single and the most eligible bachelor in Louisiana again?" Uncle Bos demanded gloomily. "He's not for you, you know."

His expression surly, he was sitting at his rusty dinette set playing with a knife he'd carved out of a razor-sharp alligator tooth while she heated his gumbo over a single flame. His sleeves were rolled so high she could see the beginnings of his many tattoos, which were angry swirls of dragons, snakes and spiders.

"No, you might say he's been knocking on mine."

He slammed a beer bottle onto the table and violently yanked the top off another. "Well, it would be a mistake to trust him. I hear he's got a new rich girlfriend."

She swallowed against the painful thickening in her suddenly dry throat.

"Name of Alicia Butler. Her daddy owns a bunch of shipyards. Banks, too. I seen her with him on television."

Instead of meeting her uncle's eyes that were much too watchful, she stared at his crucifix earring. "I know. He told me about her already."

He slammed his beer down. "I hear she's as beautiful and sweet and high class as his first wife, Noelle, who sure was a pretty thing."

Glancing away, Cici swallowed and then took a quick breath. She felt trapped suddenly and wished she was anywhere but here.

"Not that his wife ever smiled or looked happy the few times I seen her." He kicked back his chair so that he was now sprawled at a disrespectful angle.

"So, how have you been feeling, Uncle Bos?"

All four feet of his chair slammed the floor again. "I can't complain. A little tired since the chemo, but the doctors say they got it all. But then they probably always say that, the bastards."

"Maybe they're telling you the truth."

"Maybe," he agreed gloomily. "Tommy and Noonoon, they showed me all those pictures you took. I tacked a couple up in the front room."

"Yes, I saw them."

"I like the one where the vulture's about to eat those starving little girls in the desert."

"A lot of people like that one."

Everybody except her. She'd won an award for the picture, but it haunted her dreams even though she'd been able to save the girls afterwards. Still, the photo always reminded her that there were too many little girls who wouldn't be saved.

"I've quit taking pictures for a while."

"That's too bad," he said. "Why would you stop, when you're so good at it?"

Because life could get too scary.

She didn't feel like telling him that her hands shook every time she even looked at her camera case. "I needed a rest from it, that's all. It's called burnout."

"So, what did you come back here for?" he asked, a wealth of suspicion in his gravely tone.

Again, his narrow gaze was much too keen and hostile for her liking.

"I'm writing another book about Louisiana."

"That's not what I asked you, girl, and you know it. You'd be a fool if you came back because of him."

When she ignored that, too, he said, his tone caustic now, "How long you be staying?"

"It all depends."

"Not on Claiborne I hope. Don't you know that all he'll ever want from a girl with your background is to do what he did before, to get in your pants and then dump you?"

"People can change...sometimes...."

"Not so much. And not him. I know him and all his kin. And none of 'em have ever been our friend."

"Okay. We haven't so much as spoken in nine years. Can't we please..."

"You two aren't much different than you were back then. Oh, I know you think you're a professional and all because you write and took all them pictures that made you famous for a day or two. But you didn't go to college like he did. And he didn't just go to an ordinary college. He went *back East. Ivy League,*" he said sneeringly. "He's rich and powerful and conservative as hell. You're not. He lives by a set of rules that you could never cotton to, no."

"Gumbo's ready," she said, ignoring him still.

He studied her and then looked out the window in exasperation. "I don't blame you for not listenin'. There was too many times in the past, when I ignored you, too."

"I didn't come here to fight with you about Logan."

"Do you still love him?"

She swallowed tightly and didn't answer. But his eyes bored into her, and she was afraid that he saw the confusion she was determined to hide from him.

"Don't threaten him or hurt him to protect me from being a fool," she whispered.

"So that's how it is," he muttered. He spit toward a corner in disgust.

"You're wrong. I don't love him."

She bit her lips and was silent, and he made no promises to behave. But at least, he made no threats.

"After we eat some of this here gumbo, you want to take a spin with me in the swamp," he said at last. "Maybe you could help me with some traps I need to check before it gets dark."

For Uncle Bos that was as close as he was likely to come to offering to smoke the peace pipe.

"There's nothing I'd like more."

"Weird thoughts come to you when you get sick and find yourself stuck in a hospital bed," he said.

"Like what?"

"Regrets. I—I wasn't never much of an uncle to you."

"But you took me in. Where would I be if you hadn't? I wouldn't have anybody."

"Maybe you'd be better off. You wouldn't have known Claiborne."

"At least you've always been as hard on yourself as you were on me." She paused. "Just for the record, I'm glad you opened your door today."

"I resented you back then. I was through with females. I didn't think I needed any little girl messing around in my bachelor life, such that it was."

"I know."

"You'd be better off to leave this place, to leave me and Claiborne forever."

"Probably. But you and me—we don't always do what we should, now do we?"

Five

When Logan arrived at Belle Rose, and a valet parking attendant in a crisp white shirt jumped up from the steps and rushed to open Alicia's door, he wasn't surprised by the hordes. Nor was he surprised by the twinkling lights that turned the grounds into a magical fairy land or the least bit amazed when he entered the mansion with Alicia on his arm and found the house blazing with light and filled to the rafters with lively swamp pop, Cici's favorite brand of music.

All week Mrs. Dillings had been paying extravagant bills from caterers and florists and making healthy advances to various bands. If he'd raised the slightest objection to the cost of an item, his grandfather had called him, demanding that Cici, who was having the time of her life arranging everything, have her way.

Logan had done nothing but lose ground as far as Cici was concerned, and he still didn't know what she was up to. She just seemed to be moving in and taking command of his grandfather and Belle Rose, rewriting their past. In short, she was fast conquering territories that had long been his.

He was hoping tonight, somehow, that she'd do something so outrageous Grandpère would come to his senses and Logan would once again be able to assume control of his own grandfather and family again.

Logan ushered Alicia, who looked beautiful in a long backless, gold gown inside the mansion.

She stopped and glanced up at the swirling staircase and crystal chandeliers that were garlanded with fresh yellow roses. "Why, darling, your old home is even lovelier than I imagined."

Frowning because he had Cici to thank for Alicia's compliment, his gaze swept the tall vases on mantels and polished tables that overflowed with the same yellow roses as well.

"Yes. Thanks to Cici," he said.

"Talented woman."

No, dangerous.

"It reminds me of the parties my mother used to throw," Logan said. Ironically, in trying to prove her worth, his mother had destroyed it.

Those parties had stopped abruptly at his parents'

deaths when the Claibornes had found themselves mired in debt and on the brink of financial ruin due to his mother and father. Still, he remembered a younger Cici standing outside on the gallery, peeking through the windows, her round dark eyes awed and made hungry by the splendor of it all.

Grandpère was seated in the parlor holding court next to a big table stacked high with birthday presents. A dozen older women had pulled their chairs around him and were all vying for his attention. The old man appeared fit. He seemed to be having the time of his life when he looked up and saw Logan just beyond his admirers' blonde heads.

The corners of the old man's thin lips tilted upward in what appeared to be the beginnings of a smile.

Logan rushed Alicia over to meet his grandfather.

"Who is this beautiful lady?" Pierre demanded, his eyes sparkling at Alicia. When Logan introduced them, Pierre's smile warmed. A few more moments of conversation had him beaming.

"He's enjoying your company immensely. Since Grandmère died, I'm afraid the dear old fella's been lonely. And since his recent stroke, even lonelier," Logan whispered a little later. "Stay here and keep him happy a few minutes longer, while I get you something to drink, why don't you?"

"My pleasure," Alicia replied in a low voice. "I'm having fun, too. You favor him, you know."

"Chardonnay as usual?"

When she nodded in that agreeable way he found so calming, he released her elbow, nudging her a little closer to his grandfather.

Logan was on his way to the bar that had been set up in the main salon, when an uproar in the ballroom caught his attention and he turned.

At the sound of Cici's merry laughter coupled with the deeper notes of Jake's deep baritone, Logan abruptly pivoted, changing course. But when he saw Cici in a shimmering metallic sheath, her voluptuous body wrapped tightly in Jake's arms, Logan froze just outside the doorway. For a long moment Logan couldn't take his eyes off his tall, leanly muscular brother and Cici.

As the couple moved to the heavy beat of the music, he couldn't stop watching them.

Was he over-reacting or was she going after his brother now?

Whatever her motivation, Logan, who'd long regretted his past actions to both her and Jake and wanted reconciliation with his twin, suddenly felt like strangling him.

"That's some outfit." A man's voice from inside the ballroom said.

"Who are you kidding? You and every other man are looking at her legs," a woman said.

Logan clenched his fists.

"He's been gone nine years."

"The prodigal grandson. What made him come back?"

"Need you ask?" the man said. "She's hot."

"You should have seen how happy Pierre was when Jake showed up. The old man wept. So did Jake. It was so touching."

Hell.

Logan's angry gaze flicked from Cici to his dark, broad-shouldered brother, who looked too tough and strong to ever cry. Still, their grandfather's sentimentality must have affected him. Or maybe it was hard for Jake to see how much older and frailer Grandpère was.

Suddenly Logan wondered if Cici might be right in her handling of Grandpère. He was clearly thrilled about his party. Maybe the old man needed more independence and responsibility and activities rather than less. Logan had thought the old man required quiet and rest and more medical attention, but Grandpère acted like he was bored with quiet and rest. Instead of retiring to an assisted living facility, he seemed to want his active life back. He'd said he wanted to return to the office. Was that really what he should do?

"Has she interviewed you for her book?" the man standing in front of Logan asked his companion.

"Next week. We're having her to lunch. Oh, and she's bringing Pierre."

"He came with her when she interviewed me as well. She's loads of fun."

"The old man's crazy about her," the woman said. "And no wonder. She pays attention. She listens. And, yes, she's fun. It's horrible the way old people are so neglected. I don't think the poor fellow knew what to do with himself when his stroke forced him to retire. He said he got pretty gloomy until she showed up."

Jake pulled Cici close, and her laughing gaze swung to Logan. When their eyes met, Logan felt like he'd been sucker-punched.

He wasn't jealous.

Then the music stopped, and luckily he still had enough presence of mind to remember Alicia. He was turning to go after her wine, when a small, smooth hand with garish, red nails closed over his arm from behind him.

"You're late," Cici whispered against his ear, her breath as hot and soft as the satiny caresses of those searing fingertips. Her face was young and as open as it had been when she was a child.

"It was raining in New Orleans. We had trouble getting out of the city," he said.

"I missed you. So did Pierre."

"Not that that stopped you from burning up the dance floor with my brother."

"Jealous?"

"Of course not."

"You are," she whispered gently, her eyes seductively aglow. "You don't need to be."

"What?"

"It's your turn. To dance with me. But, hey, only if you want to." Again, her darkly sparkling eyes lured him.

"I have a date."

"Alicia? The merger girl?"

"That's not why I'm dating her."

"Of course."

"I left her entertaining Grandpère. I promised her a glass of wine. I'd better go."

"I'm sure your grandfather is enjoying her immensely, and she him. Jake can check on her."

"Cici, no…"

But she had already run over to Jake and was tugging at his long white sleeve. As his twin's dark head lowered over Cici's springy curls, his estranged brother looked up and then past her to Logan. Jake's eyes grew as hard and unforgiving as they'd been right before he'd slugged him and walked out. But when Cici finished talking to him, Jake turned and obediently headed out the other door, no doubt to avoid him on his way to find Alicia.

Cici returned and threaded her fingers through his.

"There's something wrong about this situation," Logan said. "I should check on Alicia myself."

"Trust me. This is a party. We're supposed to mingle a little. She came here to meet your family, didn't she? And your Alicia will love Jake. I promise. He's a do-gooder. She's a do-gooder."

"How the hell do you know so much about Alicia?"

"Research. I'm a journalist, remember."

She pulled him onto the dance floor. "Besides, what can one little dance hurt?"

Had the snake said to Eve, "What can one little apple hurt?"

Probably.

When the music resumed, he crushed Cici more tightly to him.

Even with the help of her heels, she barely came up to his shoulders. Maybe it was because she was so small and petite that her long-lashed eyes seemed so vulnerable.

He liked tall, elegant women, he reminded himself. Women who wore classy, backless gowns.

But Cici looked fresh and wholesome, and her eyes sparkled in such a way that she appeared young and playful.

He wasn't supposed to be thinking admiring thoughts about her he reminded himself. He was supposed to be trying to figure out how to get rid of her.

But it was hard to think when the effect of her body brushing against his was so electrifying. It became even harder after the music took over, and the pleasure of holding her and dancing with her stripped him of his last shred of his reason. When the first song ended, she didn't let go of him, so neither did he. One tune after another, they kept dancing. Pillars swirled past, as did the faces of those in the crowd watching them, for Cici and he were fast becoming the center of attention now.

Eyebrows were arched. Curious glances followed them. Not that Logan cared. At one point Jake even tried to cut in, but Logan ignored them all.

With each dance, Logan held Cici closer, bound her tighter, and slowly, irrevocably the voltage between them grew so strong it charged every atom in his body.

By the fourth song her eyes were closed, her cheek pressed against his shoulder, her body fused warmly to his.

When the music stopped, he was rock hard. Opening his eyes, he saw Alicia, who'd been watching them earlier, leaning on Jake's arm.

"I've got to go after Alicia," he murmured, but his husky voice lacked passion for the task.

"Yes, you really should," Cici agreed, curling a fingertip into his hair. Then another song started, and her body swayed against his. "One more dance?" she whispered as Jake turned and left the room, pulling Alicia with him.

"I'm sorry. I really do have to go to my date. I don't know what came over me. I really meant to…to stop after one dance."

"Me, too."

He bowed before leaving Cici in search of Alicia, who should have been easy to locate in her stunning, backless gown. Since she'd just left, she couldn't have had much of a head start.

But neither Alicia's slender back nor Jake's broad shoulders were anywhere to be seen.

Logan was standing at the front door about to ask the valet parkers if they'd seen his brother when his grandfather hobbled up, leaning heavily on his cane.

"Lost your date?"

"I was just about to ask the valet parkers if they'd seen her."

"Alicia wasn't feeling well, so Jake drove her home.

She told me to tell you not to worry about her, that it was just a headache."

"Thanks Grandpère."

"Is everything all right?"

Before Logan could answer, an older woman cried, "I see our birthday boy! Time to open your presents!" Then a bevy of women spilled out onto the gallery, encircled him and led him away.

When Logan dialed Alicia's cell phone, Alicia, who always picked up on the first ring, at least when he called her, didn't answer.

She had caller ID. His instinct told him she was deliberately avoiding his call. Not that he could blame her. He hadn't intended to dance with Cici more than once.

A mist was rising up from the swamp, its curling wisps threatening to envelop the grounds and soon the road with damp. If he was going after Alicia, and he was, he'd be smart to leave now before it was impossible to see. But suddenly, through the veils of mist, he thought he glimpsed a dim light come on in the top rooms of the *garçonnière*.

Had he driven Cici from the party, too, the party she'd been so excited about and had worked so hard on? Jolted from his original purpose, he took a step into the mist and then another toward the *garçonnière*.

He knew he really should go after Alicia and make sure she was all right, and he would, but first he'd tell Cici goodbye and encourage her to rejoin the party.

A waiter came up holding a tray of champagne flutes.

Logan took two. Slugging them, he smiled before replacing the flutes on the man's tray. Then, carefully, so that nobody saw him, he backed into the shadows and left the gallery.

Only when he was well away from the house and concealed by the mists, did he sprint across the thick lawn in the direction of the *garçonnière*. This time, when he reached the top of the stairs and was breathless from running, he knocked. When she didn't answer immediately, instead of barging inside as before, he forced himself to pace the landing.

When she still didn't answer, he beat his fist against the door again and yelled her name. "I know you're in there!"

"Coming," she said at last.

Still, it was several more minutes before she finally pushed her door open. Not that she even looked at him. Busy dressing, she bent her head and shrugged into a black T-shirt.

"Wonderful party," he said.

She wore the black T-shirt and dark jeans, but because she'd only lit a single lamp and the *garçonnière* was full of shadows and her body was back lit, revealing her slender shape which seemed so sexy, he sucked in a breath.

"I'm sorry I made trouble between you and your date," she said, turning away as she tucked the T-shirt into her jeans.

He inhaled sharply again. "That was my fault," he said, feeling awkward around her.

When he jerked his eyes from her body, he saw her dress on the floor where she'd tossed it, the garment sparkling up at him as if with wicked glee.

Cici, her slim back to him now, was squatting on her haunches—well-shaped haunches encased in tight black denim, too. Leaning over, exposing more of her delectably rounded butt, she began to dig through the chaos of her shoes that spilled out of her closet into her bedroom.

Heat engulfed him, which was ridiculous. He was thirty-five, not some lust-driven teenager. Still, his heart began to slam in slow, painful strokes.

Ignoring him, she shoved bare toes into a jogging shoe and then began rummaging for its mate.

"What do you think you're doing?" he demanded.

"I'm taking the pirogue out in the swamp."

"At this time of night? Are you crazy?"

"What does it look like?"

"You're supposed to be Grandpère's hostess."

"I'm supposed to be a lot of things." She was trembling as she threw her shoes about. "Thanks to you, I need some air. Some space. Lots of it."

So Alicia wasn't the only woman he'd upset. He stepped into her bedroom. "I don't want you out there. All alone. In danger."

"Since when is my putting myself in danger any of your business?"

"There's ground fog. You could get lost."

"Isn't that what you want? Me gone? So, big deal! I'm going!"

"Anything could happen."

"So? I'm a big girl. I can handle myself."

"Something might eat you." So, he was probably exaggerating. Still…

"Hey, there. If this scares you I won't tell you about the time I had a pilot drop me off at the Zambezi River on a dirt strip, and my contact didn't show up because he'd been gut shot and was on an operating table. The plane flew off, and I was all alone in a jungle and lions were roaring."

She laughed and then stopped. "Sorry." She paused. "If I'm feeling a little hysterical, it's because I'm a lot more scared of you than I could ever be of the swamp I practically grew up in. You were right. I shouldn't have come back. But now that I'm here, I've got to figure out how to deal with what I'm feeling. I think best in the swamp."

He swallowed. "Cici, the reason I followed you out here is because I don't want my actions to ruin the party for you."

"Oh, really? Is that why?" Again she laughed, but not gaily.

"I shouldn't have danced…"

"Do you think you can lie to yourself and to me forever? You want me. I could see it and feel it on the dance floor. I can feel it now, too. You're wondering if we're still as good together as we were in the past."

"Why do you always push?"

"Is it me pushing? Or is it something inside us?"

He turned away from her.

"Something like sex," she said. "Let's be honest. You're a man, so, naturally, you want sex, and you think you don't stand a chance tonight with your Alicia, who's probably mad as hell at both of us—and I don't blame her. You think it'll be easier to get it here from me than from her. Plus, it'll be of the no strings variety, 'cause you're who you are, and I'm who I am. And no strings and something strange is just the thing to tempt most men…especially hypocrites, like you, who can't even admit what they feel."

"No, listen…"

"No, *you* listen! Why don't you do us both a favor and go chase your tame Alicia, who's so perfect for you? I'm sure she's more than willing to believe any lie you choose to tell her."

"I don't care about Alicia," he whispered, shocked by the truth of that statement even as he said it. "I want you. Not her. There! I admitted it! Are you happy?"

"You'd say anything—"

"I want you! I've tried not to."

When Cici stood up, both shoes on now, he had to strain to see her expression in the dim light. "You tried not to? How do you think that makes me feel? We've done this before. We made a lot of people miserable, including ourselves."

"And I thought you liked living dangerously."

"Not tonight. Not with you. Sure, in the past I've taken a few risks. Mostly because I was too foolish and young to know what I was doing. Like that time I was telling you about in Zimbabwe. That happened just after…after you'd dumped me and…and I'd left."

The incredible pain in her eyes hit them hard. "But this is different. Maybe I've had my fill of my heart being broken. Maybe I just want to write for some local newspaper and settle down to a simple, predictable life with a nice boring guy who loves me and is sweet to me. Maybe I've finally realized that what I want, which is happily ever after with some boring guy, is impossible with you."

He leaned his shoulders back against the jamb of her door. She'd given him his out. He should take it.

"So, like I said, go. Do us both a favor, and spill your heart out to your pretty, proper, rich Alicia. Like I said, she'll forgive you."

When he said nothing, she took a step toward him. "Damn it, go!" When he didn't, she took a quick breath.

He stared at her, willing himself to do as she said and go. But he couldn't.

The tension built until the humming in his blood was so loud he was afraid she could hear it. Finally, he crossed the room and pulled her into his arms. The instant his hands wrapped her, she shivered, her heat and passion flowing through him like a contagion. Pulling her closer, he shuddered.

"Go," she whispered huskily even as her hands clung to him. "You're scaring me."

"You didn't used to be afraid of anything."

"Not even of hungry lions." She laughed weakly.

"Funny, I value my life so much now that I'm afraid to pick up my camera, afraid of you…afraid of feeling all this…"

She didn't look afraid. Her cheeks were flushed. Her eyes glowed. Every inch of her felt electric and silky and hot.

"I'm afraid of dying now…I think because I want to live so much," she said.

The mists were seeping into her wide-open windows, swirling around them. In the distance he could hear the mating cry of a wild bull alligator in the swamp.

"Kiss me," he said, his voice rougher, needier.

Then, too impatient to wait when she remained frozen, he claimed her mouth, driving his tongue deeply inside her with a violence that scared him even more than it frightened her. His hands slipped beneath her T-shirt and unhooked her bra.

"You taste delicious. Like champagne," she said.

He should slow it down, but he couldn't.

With a shudder, his arms wound tighter and he forced her closer.

"Two glasses. Couldn't resist," he said. "Not much really."

His breath was loud and harsh now. He wanted to possess her with every cell in his being, and he was fast losing control.

Besides pressuring her, what he was doing was probably wrong on a dozen levels. But when she began kissing him back, hesitantly at first, her lips were sweet and hot and quivering beneath his. Then when she gave him all she had, he was soon driven past all thought and reason.

As if shocked by the pleasure he gave her, she let out a startled cry.

His arms wound tighter. He had to have her. And it was more than a physical need.

To hell with right and wrong and sanity, he thought as his need blazed ever higher until it consumed him.

"Did you bring a condom this time?" she whispered, sounding as frantic with passion as he felt.

Six

Cici was being stupid, and she hated that because she always regretted being stupid later. Logan Claiborne was the one man she should never sleep with because he held the key to a part of herself she wanted to protect forever.

So why had she made sure he had plenty of condoms? So why was she lying naked on his bed with him sprawled heavily on top of her? They'd barely started making love, but already, with his every caress, with his every kiss, he was stripping her soul so bare that she felt like she was crashing and shattering and flying into a million jagged pieces.

After he was finished with her tonight, would she ever be able to feel whole again?

Logan's mouth traveled from her throat down her belly, across her scar, pausing there and kissing it so tenderly that she wept.

Her breath stopped and she began to quiver. In a flash she remembered holding their precious son in her arms that one time.

Their son. The only human being she'd ever loved half so much as that darling child was Logan.

Only when Logan's lips moved ever lower, and he found her softest, most secret flesh and began stroking her there, could she stop thinking about their lost baby and breathe again. But soon, too soon, he had her emotions in turmoil again and she was, clinging and shaking, but by then he was, too.

Wet and ready for him, even before he spread her legs and laved her long and deeply, she drove her finger through his hair and drew his head closer, moaning as his skillful mouth and deft tongue licked her and sent shiver after shiver hotly pulsing through her, evoking forbidden longings she hadn't felt in years.

Hadn't wanted to feel!

She bit her lips and tightened her fists in an attempt to fight her fierce pleasure. But it didn't work because what she felt was too powerful.

A younger, more naive Cici had imagined herself madly in love with him in this same room. She'd lost that happy, glowing feeling at immense cost to her soul, because he'd thrown her away. To save his brother, he'd claimed.

She did not want to be in love with him again. He was too cold and logical. Too cruel. He'd shown her once that he was a man who always did what was best for him or his family.

But what if she was no more in control of her easily bruised heart than she had ever been?

Maybe her fierce anger and the self-destructive hatred that had driven her to taunt death had been the dark side of her love for him. What if she was willing to risk anything to be his, willing to pay any price for another chance?

When his tongue found *the zone* and began licking small, satiny circles, a series of wild thrills such as she had never known rippled through her. Opening wider, she arched her pelvis against his mouth.

The *garçonnière* was an utterly dark cocoon. Nine years ago, in this same bed, she'd been a virgin. Again she reminded herself that he'd taken her and then had cruelly discarded her.

What would he do tomorrow? With these worries in her mind, the hotter her passion grew as Logan claimed her with his mouth and tongue, the more her emotions spiraled into fear.

She'd borne him a son with hair the exact dark shade of Logan's. When the doctors had told her that they'd lost her little boy, she'd asked to hold him. After his funeral, she'd locked her terrible secret in her heart, intending to keep it there forever.

Until tonight, when Logan had walked into the ballroom and looked at her, his gaze as lost and feverishly dark as her own broken soul, she'd believed herself incapable of ever loving him or ever sharing her profound loss with him. Now old emotions were reigniting.

He spread her legs wider. His tongue delved deeper, and she moaned as the throbbing excitement built, spreading like a ravaging flame that devoured every part of her until she burst in a final explosion and became completely his.

Breathing hard, she shut her eyes.

Do we choose those we love? Or are they a gift? Hadn't he always possessed her soul?

"For nine years I've wanted to do that again," he whispered, "to taste you, to hear you moan like that. To give you pleasure."

At his husky words and tender embrace, she held onto him tightly, not daring to let herself believe anything he said.

It was just sex. "Don't say things we'll both regret."

"The last thing I want is for you to regret anything about tonight," he murmured. Then he moved up to straddle her.

"No regrets. I promise. I'm a big girl now."

She wrapped her arms around his neck and drew his mouth to hers.

"I was a fool nine years ago," he said.

"So was I."

"You were only naive, but I was cruel. Can you ever forgive me?"

"That will depend on what you do next."

"I don't want to hurt you like that ever again."

Then don't, she thought as he put on a condom.

When he finished, she kissed his lips in a long, soul-shattering kiss. When she felt his sheathed manhood probe at the velvety folds of her secret entrance, she opened her legs, and he plunged—deep and true. For a long moment, he simply held her and was still, and she savored the sensation of being joined to him.

Oh, the pleasure, the immense pleasure that only being with him could give her.

"I promise not to hurt you," he whispered.

She nodded, not really believing him. After all, he'd promised such things before.

Slowly his hands began to caress her hair. Then his mouth brushed across her lips, her cheek, before moving down to her throat.

Bending over her, he began to move with her in such abandon, she was soon crying out.

Wrapping her arms around his shoulders, she arched her body higher and higher, meeting his every thrust. Their passion built, and she surrendered completely, exploding with him.

Afterward, she buried her face against his shoulder and held on to him for a long time, wishing, no, longing for so much more than a man like him could ever give a woman like her.

"What are you thinking?" he asked, his arms tightening around her as he brushed her hair out of her eyes.

The confused emotions in her heart made her suddenly shy. "Sex makes people, especially women who are fools like me, do and feel the craziest things. I could write a book on the subject."

"Please don't. Not if you're going to write about me."

She giggled. "You're a prude. You know that, don't you?"

"Conservative."

"Not in bed." She smoothed her fingers through his chocolate dark hair. When the thick lock fell back over his brow immediately, she pushed it back again and smiled. "Only afterwards, do you get uptight, when you fall back into being your true self."

"My true self? Who the hell is that? Do we ever know our true selves? For years I did what my grandfather taught me to think was best for the family."

"I found mine behind a camera."

"Lucky you."

"Or not. I saw too much pain. I can't even pick up a camera now."

"You didn't answer my original question," he said. "What were you thinking a while ago."

"I don't know. I've forgotten."

"Then I'll make love to you again, in the hope that you'll remember."

"Will that be your only reason?" she teased.

As soon as he began to kiss her, the moist warmth of his mouth and tongue had her shivering in newly heightened awareness of him, maybe because the first time they'd made love tonight, he'd broken down all the walls of her resistance and she was wide open to him now. As before he swept her on a dark tide of passion to the other side of the moon, to a wild place that was theirs alone, a place where she forgot herself and might have whispered desperate, foolish things against his ear, but fortunately in that last shuddering moment, she remembered all that divided them.

In the past he'd hurt her, and it had taken her years to get over it. Who was to say that although she was older and wiser, it couldn't happen again? No matter how close to loving him she felt, she could not let herself succumb.

"I never thought I'd feel like this again," he said afterward, triumphant that he'd taken her to such heights, maybe because his manhood was still embedded deep within her and she was clinging to him fiercely.

She couldn't think with him inside her. She felt too warm and snug, too safe, and such feelings were not to be trusted.

"I have a lot of making up to do for how I treated you, don't I?" he said.

"An entire lifetime wouldn't begin to suffice," she said. "So we agree then, that you owe me?"

He pulled her even closer if that were possible. "Big time. I will make it up to you. I swear. I don't care if it takes an entire lifetime."

Her heart caught as she eased herself out of his arms. Not that she was about to let herself hope for anything from him, for she had learned that hope, not fear, not grief, was the cruelest of emotions. And men like him would say anything in bed. The truth would come in the morning.

When he yanked the sheets around them and wrapped her in his arms again, she thought about the dark-haired little boy they'd lost, the little boy he didn't know about...yet.

Then, soon, because of Logan's body heat and his tenderness, the image dissolved. For the first time in years, she felt almost safe even though she knew she shouldn't, not with him, not ever with him.

Despite her misgivings, she fell into a deep, fathomless sleep.

Logan woke up first, wrapped in the warmth of a beautiful woman, the one woman he should not be with, their tangled sheets reeking of steamy sex. Alert, in the dazzling light of a new morning, he froze.

It was a helluva shock to find Cici's head resting so trustingly on his shoulder. Not that it should have been. What did last night mean?

Had he been lying to himself when he'd been so determined to send her packing? Remembering how tenderly she'd held him each time after they'd made love, he winced. She was sweet, as sweet as she'd been as a girl. What did she want? Need? Had he ever thought of that once?

Had he simply used her?

She deserved better.

Hell, any woman deserved better.

Even as the memory of her mouth all over his body stung him, he told himself she couldn't possibly fit into his life. Last night hadn't changed anything. And yet….

Slowly, trying not to wake her, he shifted his weight. Gently placing her head onto a pillow, he had eased himself almost to the edge of the bed before she stirred. Rolling over, she faced him. With a happy little sigh, she tenderly traced her fingertips down the length of his arm.

"Logan," she whispered dreamily.

"Right here," he murmured, trying to resist the instant high voltage coupled with the unaccountable tenderness he felt for her.

Long lashes fluttered again, revealing dark eyes glimmering with too much hope and affection. "I thought you'd be long gone."

Hell.

He should have been. He didn't know what to say. He only knew he didn't want to hurt her any more than he had to. "I'm where I want to be."

"Really?"

"Really!" It *had* been heaven lying in her arms. That part was undeniable. Determined to leave as fast as possible, he threw off the sheet and then couldn't help but admire her beautiful body. And her smile. She had an incredible smile. Then he frowned when he saw the vague, moon-shaped scar on her abdomen that he'd first noticed the afternoon he'd barged in on her. Without thinking, his hand lightly traced the white curve.

"What happened to you here?" he murmured, growing more concerned when she trembled.

Her eyes snapped open. Meeting his, they grew huge and confused, so painfully confused, and then tears, real tears filled them. Before he knew what had happened, she was turning away from him.

"What's wrong?" he demanded. "You've got to tell me." Gently, he placed his hands on her shoulders and felt her body trembling even harder.

Her face was pale. Her lips quivered when she turned toward him again. "It doesn't matter," she said. "At least, not right now, when you probably have a million things to do."

Alarm filling him because she was so passionately upset, seemingly for no reason, he pulled her closer. He felt guilty as hell, wondering if this fresh emotional turmoil could possibly be his fault.

"Tell me," he said, forgetting everything he needed to attend to in New Orleans and concentrating on her.

"I tried to tell you…once…"

But, as she was about to begin, his cell phone began ringing, interrupting her.

"Go on," he said, ignoring it.

But his ringing phone had her distracted. "Hadn't you better answer that first?" she said.

"It can wait."

"No. Go ahead. It doesn't really matter. You know how easily women become emotional. You have important things to do."

She turned away, and he reluctantly lunged for his phone.

No sooner had Logan said hello, than Mitchell Butler blasted him. "What the hell did you do to my daughter?"

"What's wrong with her?"

"She becomes very upset every time I ask her a question or mention your name."

"Okay," he said, feeling guilty as he waited for more.

"No! It's not okay, and until I find out what you did to her, the merger's off."

"I can explain." But could he?

"Then get your sorry ass back to town and do so." Mitchell hung up.

"What's wrong?" Cici asked. "Was that Alicia?"

"Her father. He's calling off the merger. I need to call Hayes."

She nodded, her expression cool, as he punched in Hayes's number.

Hayes answered on the first ring. Logan didn't bother to identify himself. "Butler just called. He wants a meeting."

"I know. This afternoon. At one sharp. He says the merger's off. Mind if I ask what the hell's going on?"

"I can be in New Orleans in an hour or so. I'll explain everything then."

"Must have been some party. Did Miss Bellefleur throw you another one of her curve balls? Did you strike out or hit a home run?"

"Don't hold your breath until you get the update." Logan flipped his phone shut and whirled on Cici.

"Sorry about all that," he muttered, feeling bad about how he'd treated Alicia. Suddenly he was too aware that their lives were on opposite tracks. "I guess I'd better get back to New Orleans and start putting out all the fires I've started."

"Sure," Cici whispered, but her voice caught. And her face was paper white. "I'll make you some coffee and toast, so you won't have to stop for breakfast on your way home."

"You were telling me what happened to you," he said as he grabbed his slacks off the floor.

"Not now, when your world's in pieces because of me and you're in such a hurry," she whispered, her voice sounding sad and lost as she turned away.

"But I want to know happened to you," he said.

"It doesn't matter. Like I said, it's obvious you have truly important concerns this morning."

"Cici…"

Ignoring him, she opened a can of coffee.

"Well, if she wouldn't tell him, she wouldn't tell him. He had to respect her reasons and let it go, at least, for now.

He dressed hurriedly. Not that he didn't look a mess with both his shirt and slacks so wrinkled they looked like he'd slept on them. Hell, he probably had.

"Last night was great," he said.

"Right," she said, popping two pieces of bread into her toaster.

"Incredible," he persisted.

"I'm glad you feel that way…if you do."

"What the hell is that supposed to mean?"

"It means whatever happened last night, this morning…these phone calls are your reality."

"Hell."

"Then tell me I'm wrong."

He couldn't even look at her, much less lie to her, so he stared out the window for a long minute while that telltale nerve in his jaw jumped painfully. "Look, I do have to get back to New Orleans as fast as possible."

"Of course. I know." Her teeth chattering, she wrapped her red robe more tightly around herself and concentrated on her toaster. Frowning, she began to tap her nails on the counter. "Damn it, why are appliances always so slow?"

Hoping to dispel the distinct chill in the morning air, he smiled and said, "It's because you're watching it."

She didn't look up from her toaster. He could tell she was in an even bigger hurry than he was for him to be gone.

"Hey, would you quit worrying about my toast? I can eat on the road."

"I'm not…worrying…about your stupid toast. Or you. I'm thinking about my looming deadline. I need to work. You're not the only one with a life, you know. I need to get some writing done. No more procrastinating. The last thing I need is *this* distraction."

"So, that's all I am now to you, a distraction?"

"I can always hope, can't I?" she said quietly.

"Me, too."

When his toast popped out, she jumped. Then clenching her fists at her sides, she took a deep, determined breath before plucking the two pieces out and tossing them onto a plate.

"So, the sooner I leave, the happier you'll be?" he said.

"What do you want me to say? What other choice do I have here?" Her tone and gaze were bleak. "You have your world of mergers and wealth. I have mine. Nine years ago I didn't fully understand such realities. I do now. Last night was great. But it's over. So, go. You're free. No strings attached."

The woman who'd writhed in his arms with total abandon, his Cici with the sparkling eyes, was gone. In her place was a woman with a bad case of bed hair, an ashen complexion and dull, swollen eyes. He'd made her unhappy—again.

Obviously, she was right about their situation, but for some harebrained, illogical reason, this thought didn't make him happy at all. He hated upsetting her.

"Eat," she commanded gently. "Then go. For both our sakes. Oh, and lock the door on your way out."

"So, you're saying last night was a mistake?"

She was padding toward the bathroom, but at his question, she stopped and turned. "You didn't look all that happy when I woke up, so for you…I think it was. So, I'm saying don't ever knock on my door again… Not unless…"

"Unless what?"

Her warm eyes fixed on his face and held his gaze for a long, intense moment.

"You're smart. You figure it out."

He wanted to rush across the room and pull her close. He wanted to crush her to him and never let her go. He wanted to stay and drink coffee and talk to her for hours. Which was ridiculous.

Instead, he swallowed. She was right. They'd had sex. Nothing more. Shrugging, he turned. Then bracing himself, he walked out the door.

But with every purposeful step he took away from her, his feet felt heavier. And so did his heart. He wanted to hear about everything she'd done when she'd been away.

The merger he'd worked so hard on was going up in flames, and all he could think about was Cici's wounded feelings and his own leaden emotion as he faced his life without her. What the hell was wrong with him?

Seven

A front was sweeping in from Texas. The gloomy morning matched Logan's mood as he stood at the front door of one of Jake's new houses, talking to Jake's real estate agent.

Cici. As Logan had driven to New Orleans, he'd kept seeing her in her red robe with her messy hair tumbling about her face in those crazy tufts, with her brilliant blue eyes lit by despair and hope. Even then, she'd seemed utterly beautiful.

And once away from her, his body had reacted viscerally to her absence. With every mile, the lump in his throat had grown and his chest had tightened until his heart had seemed squeezed by a vise. He hated the way they'd parted.

More than anything he'd wanted to turn back and floor the gas pedal. How could it feel so insane to be leaving her, when what was really insane was his tense longing to be with her? Why couldn't he focus on the merger?

"Thanks for your help," Logan said aloud, trying to sound normal, as he handed Jake's real estate broker his card. "So, if you see my brother, you'll be sure to tell him to call any of these numbers. Mr. Mitchell Butler wants to make sure his daughter's all right, and we think Jake was the last person with her."

"Then she's safe and sound," the man said reassuringly. "Jake's the most trustworthy guy in the whole world. But you should know that—you're his twin."

"Right." Logan nodded. Then the door slammed, and Logan found himself standing alone on the porch of one of the newly built houses Jake and his investors were constructing in the Lower Ninth Ward.

With solar panels on the roof as well as an escape hatch in case of another flood, the home was sleek and modern. The first floor topped the required eight feet above sea level by at least a foot or two.

Logan leaned against the railing. He had thirty minutes to get to the emergency meeting Mitchell Butler had called in Hayes's office, and he didn't have anything new to give to Mitchell.

Still, Logan took a second or two to study the rest of the half dozen new houses his brother had under construction. Jake had certainly made something of himself. He wasn't just rich; he was making a difference. Like the house Logan was standing on, all Jake's houses were modern, affordable, green, and well-designed and well-built, too.

Other than Jake's project and a few others like it, not nearly enough progress had been made rebuilding neighborhoods like this since the hurricanes. Vast empty fields and broken roads and a few trailers were all that was left of the once vital community that had been flooded when the nearby levee had been breached several years ago.

Logan forced his mind to Alicia. He didn't blame her for not answering her phone, but if he couldn't reach her, how could he appease Mitchell before their meeting about the merger?

Earlier Logan had dropped by the building in the Quarter where Alicia lived. Her doorman had been only too happy to inform him that she'd come home early this morning with a man who looked a whole lot like Logan, that she'd packed a bag, and that the two of them had left almost immediately.

"He had his arm around her. He seemed to be comforting her. Until you showed up, I thought he was you."

So, where were they?

Logan punched in Alicia's cell phone number, but as it rang, a vision of Cici naked in bed beneath him last night sprang into his mind. God, she'd felt so deliciously hot he couldn't stop thinking about her.

All morning as he'd searched for Alicia and Jake, Cici had been on his mind. He kept remembering her taste and the thrill of her soft, wet lips when she'd gone down on her knees to pleasure him. He got hard every time he thought about it, which was all the time, damn it.

Last night had been wonderful. Everything had been great after they'd started making love until he'd awakened to sobering reality this morning. Even so, he hadn't been gone from her five minutes before he'd wanted to turn his Lexus around and drive right back and reassure her.

He had his own life, even if it was a mess at present. He couldn't let himself care about Cici Bellefleur. But suppose he did care.

As Logan raced down the steps to his Lexus, he dialed Alicia's cell phone. When her voice mail picked up again, he snapped his phone shut. Clearly, she wasn't ready to be found. At least not by him.

Who could blame her?

He was jamming his key in the ignition, when his own phone rang. Finally, he thought, sure it was Alicia.

Hayes spoke instead. "Mitch just walked in. You'd better get the hell over here."

"He's early. It's only twelve-thirty. Our meeting isn't until one."

"He's here. He says you're late. He says the meeting's supposed to start now."

"He always thinks all meetings should start whenever he shows up. He's being unreasonable—as usual."

"I don't think he likes you very much this morning, either. Would somebody please tell me what the hell is going on?"

"Mitch thinks I hurt Alicia."

"Well, did you?"

"Not on purpose. Alicia won't talk to me, so I don't know exactly what is wrong with her."

"Is Miss Bellefleur involved in any of this?"

"I don't want to talk about her."

"Okay. So, sounds like she's involved. Not good." He paused. "Mitchell just told me he has another offer—a very attractive offer from J.L. Brown. So, where does this leave our merger?"

"You'd better ask Mitchell."

The door of the dress shop closed behind Cici with a tinkle of merry, silvery bells. Her emotions had been in such turmoil ever since Logan had left, she'd been unable to think, much less focus on her book. So, she'd driven into town on an errand for Noonoon and to check a book out of the library for Pierre. And, now after seeing the blue dress in the shop window, she was shopping to distract herself.

Besides, she'd been desperate to get away from the telephone because despite everything she'd said to the contrary to Logan, she'd longed for him to call. If everybody else on the planet hadn't phoned to say how much he or she had loved the party, maybe she wouldn't have noticed Logan's neglect quite as much. But every time the phone had rung, she'd driven herself crazy wishing it was him.

If only she could stop thinking about him, stop wishing he'd acted differently this morning.

Stupid. She knew what kind of man he was.

The elderly saleslady at the cash register looked up and smiled. "May I help you?"

"That dress in the window. It caught my eye. The blue one with the full skirt."

"The sweet little sundress?"

"I was wondering if you had it in my size."

"You're a four, aren't you, dear?"

"How did you know?"

Cici's gaze was then drawn to a red lace bra and matching thong.

"Sexy, aren't they? Just the things to win a man." The saleslady smiled at her dreamily. "I used to be a four...and wear naughty underthings...but that was many, many years ago."

Maybe so, but her step was as light as a girl's as she hurried to the rack in the back and found the blue dress Cici liked in a four.

In no time Cici had the dress on and was staring at herself in a long, gilt-edged mirror lit by spring sunshine.

Twirling, she imagined the warmth in Logan's eyes when he saw her in this dress. Would he approve? Was it demure enough?

Forget him. He's in New Orleans with rich, perfect Alicia.

You don't know that. Not for sure.

For almost sure. She's beautiful. She has a fortune. Then there's a merger in jeopardy. You can't begin to compete with her. Or his real life.

The bodice clung to Cici's breasts and made her waist look tiny. The blue skirt floated, swirling around her legs and hips every time she took a step.

He hadn't gone after Alicia last night.

The dress was sexy, but classy, conservative, too. Not really her at all. *Well, at least it was sexy.*

"Cinderella," the saleslady said. "You're Cinderella in that dress. Minus the glass slippers."

A sign?

Cinderella *had* married her prince.

"I'll take it," Cici said. "Next I want to try on that red bra and thong."

"I have a couple of other dresses that you'd be equally stunning in. Would you like to see them, too?"

Later that afternoon at the *garçonnière,* Cici, who was three demure dresses richer, removed her bright nail polish and pulled her hair neatly back, tying it at the nape with a blue ribbon. She put on her new blue dress and turned around, eyeing herself in her mirror.

Satisfied with her maidenly appearance, if only because she believed it to be more to Logan's taste, she picked up her briefcase and her computer. Then she walked over to Belle Rose and let herself into the library where she intended to do research for her book.

A dress and a hairdo won't make any difference, her little voice taunted. *You're still who you are. Swamp Girl.*

Ignoring the voice, she went to Pierre's shelves and began pulling books down that had to do with her subject. Not that she really wanted to read them. Noonoon told Pierre she'd come over, and he came downstairs and took the book she'd gotten for him and began to read on the couch.

While she forced herself to work, he intermittently napped and read. She took a break, and they had tea and crackers together. But all the while, her mind was only half on her work because she was secretly waiting for her phone to ring and for Logan to say he was missing her as much as she missed him.

Crazy. They'd had sex. Meaningless sex.

The first time her cell rang, she jumped for it. But it was only her Uncle Bos calling to say he was having a bad day, which meant he was having a very bad day since he wasn't a whiner and never called her, and would she stop over later and maybe tend bar if he was still too tired. Of course, she said yes.

Cici stood up and went to the window. Looking out at the gray wet, she told herself that she had to quit thinking about last night, about how wonderful she'd felt in Logan's arms.

Clearly it was over. Clearly last night hadn't meant anything to him. Therefore, it couldn't mean anything to her.

An hour later she was hard at work, taking notes feverishly in an attempt not to think about Logan when the phone rang again. This time it was her agent.

"How would you like to do a feature story on the bombings in Egypt near the pyramids? You always said you wanted to see the pyramids. This would be just the thing…and a *feature*…a *feature*…that is, if you're ready to pick up your camera again."

Part of her wanted to run away from last night, from what she'd done, from what she was afraid she felt for Logan. A monthlong shoot hiding behind her camera far, far away, focusing on other people's misery would be just the thing to take her mind off her own recklessly foolish behavior here at home.

"I have a deadline," she said because, of course, like any self-destructive, infatuated idiot, she was too fixed on the object of her torment to consider leaving him.

"What if I could get you an extension? I think this project would be worth your while." Her agent named the generous fee the feature would pay. "Can you afford to pass it up?"

Not really. This is your career. Logan's probably with Alicia right now. So, for once, do the smart thing. Pick up your camera again. Leave him. Run. Don't risk this getting out of hand.

Cici remembered the night she'd held their little son in that sterile hospital room. His skin had felt so thin and papery, and yet soft, too. He'd seemed so fragile and broken. And she'd felt like the loneliest human being in the universe when she'd finally kissed his cool brow goodbye.

She really should run. Because if she wasn't careful, she had no doubt Logan would hurt her again, maybe even worse than the first time.

* * *

Exhausted, Logan sat hunched behind his desk, which was littered with dozens of documents that would never be signed by Mitchell or himself. Even after hours of negotiation today, the merger was dead.

A year of work, hopes and dreams were down the drain. His future with Alicia was over as well. So, what?

Logan ran his hands through his hair. Curiously, he was too tired to care. Maybe tomorrow, the loss of it all would hit him. but then maybe not. All day he'd felt different, curiously free of his seething ambition. Things that always mattered to him more than anything, hadn't gripped him.

Someone knocked on the door of his outer office, and he heard Mrs. Dillings greet whomever it was much too cheerfully for it to be so late in the day. And on a Sunday.

She was amazing. She'd come in early. Did she never tire?

Then his own intercom buzzed. "It's your brother," she said in a calm tone, as if Jake's reappearance at Claiborne Energy at such a disastrous moment on a Sunday evening after an absence of nine years was a matter of course.

Forgetting the merger, Logan sprang to his feet, dashed to the door and threw it open just as Jake was striding toward it. When his twin's hard gaze met his, Logan stiffened, but only for a second.

Relaxing, Logan grinned. "You're not going to hit me this time, are you?"

Jake smiled as he thrust his big hand toward him. Without hesitation Logan shook it heartily.

"Welcome home. It's been too long," he said.

"Much too long. What can I say? We Claibornes are a stubborn bunch. Unforgiving to a fault."

"It's genetic," Logan said. "I was high-handed and completely out of line."

"To say the least. Still, I stayed away too long. I guess we both take after the old man."

"In any case, I'm sorry for manipulating your life. And Cici's."

"Hey, I guess I should have been used to it. But what about Cici?" Jake's smile died. "After the way you two danced together, I can't help wondering if she's forgiven you, too?"

"Not yet, but maybe I'm working on it." Logan paused. "Care to sit down?"

"Another time. This will just take a moment." Jake was smiling, but he seemed tense.

Logan shut the door.

"The reason I came by," Jake said, "or one of the reasons is that I know you've been calling Alicia last night and again today." He hesitated. "Because I was with her when you did, you see. So, I know she hasn't returned your calls."

"Is she okay?"

"She's fine. But she says it's over between you two, or rather that it never was. And I wanted to know if that is true."

Logan inhaled. "If she says so."

"What about you? Would you care if she started seeing someone else?"

"Meaning you, I suppose."

"She wants nothing to do with me. She says it's too soon. And that I'm the last man she'd ever date because I remind her too much of you."

"Sorry. I'm afraid I behaved badly toward her at the party."

"I explained about you and Cici."

"I should have explained things myself, but I was in the middle of them and didn't understand them too well myself."

"You never did. You loved Cici, you know. You were just too damn stubborn or arrogant to admit it."

"Well, I wish Alicia every happiness. You will tell her that if you see her or talk to her before I do, won't you?"

"Right now, she's not taking my calls."

Jake soon turned their conversation to a safer topic, their grandfather's health, and the next ten minutes were spent pleasantly. When they parted, they shook hands again and wished each other well.

It would take a while to mend the rift of years and renew their former emotional closeness, Logan thought as he turned off the lights so he could leave, too. But, at least they'd made a small start.

Cici was eating a sandwich for supper at her kitchen counter while she watched the news on her television.

The breakup of the merger between Butler Shipyards and Claiborne Energy was such big news, it was on every channel.

She was grabbing her purse on her way out to T-Bos's Bar when her cell rang.

"I want to see you," Logan said, his voice so deep and dark, the energy in it charged her.

"I saw the news about the merger. Sounds like you had a rough day. I'm sorry."

"Are you busy tonight?"

"What am I? Your consolation prize."

"Hell, I don't know."

"What kind of answer is that?"

"What kind of question is that?"

All day she'd thought about his kisses and lovemaking until she'd felt he'd branded her as his own. And he didn't even know why he was calling her.

"I was on my way out when you called," she said.

"I can't quit thinking about you."

She couldn't, either. "So what? Bad habits are hard to break."

"Cici…"

"So, how's Alicia?"

"I haven't spoken to her."

"Why?"

"Because she won't talk to me, that's why. But you might say she sent a message to me through a friend. It's over between us."

"Oh, you're feeling lonely and vulnerable as a result.

Which is why you're calling me. And like a stupid sap I answer. So, you think maybe I'll make myself available to you again?"

"No. That's not it."

"Of course, you won't admit it. You're a man. Last night turned you on. If this is about sex…you wanting it…thinking you can get it from me…and not being able to get it from your fancy girlfriend…and nothing else…"

"Cici, I do want to see you. Forget Alicia. Like I said—that's over."

"Look, you didn't call me all day. So, it's a little late now, okay?"

"I thought about you all day…all the damn day. Does that count?"

"Why should I care?"

"I thought about you until I'm sick of thinking about you! I couldn't call because I was dealing with Mitchell Butler and his unreasonable demands. Which were many. Then I was stuck in meetings with the board doing damage control after he trashed our merger."

"Poor little rich multimillionaire. Or is it billionaire? Well, I can't see you. Okay? Not tonight. Because I've made other plans. My uncle's sick, and I promised to help him out."

"Tomorrow, then?"

"Not tomorrow, either."

"Why?"

"I have a life, you know, and so do you as you clearly demonstrated this morning. Oh, and there's my deadline.

You should thank me. I'm letting you off the hook. I'm trying to be smart and logical for a change. And that's not easy for me."

"Cici…"

"Goodbye!"

She hung up on him. When her phone rang again, and she saw it was him, she leaned against her counter with clenched fists. She felt all mixed up, wild to see him on the one hand, but scared to death where it would lead.

All day she'd felt almost sick with longing for him, and then he'd finally called. But what was different between them? He wanted her for sex, and she was afraid she was already too involved to resist him.

Better to stop now, if she still could.

A least ten minutes passed before she got herself together enough to walk into her bathroom and splash cold water onto her hot face. After bemoaning the fact she looked absolutely awful whenever she was this upset, she carefully touched up her makeup. Then with a swish of her blue skirts, she marched down her stairs with her head held high.

Nobody at T-Bos's could know that her heart was breaking tonight. Not for Logan Claiborne. They'd think her a fool, which she probably was.

Eight

Logan pulled up beside Cici's Miata which was of course parked squarely in the middle of at least thirty or more big black motorcycles. His gaze drifting over cobras and rattlesnakes and angry streaks of red flames painted on the various bikes, Logan cut his engine. Not that he was eager to get out of his Lexus and face these bikers from hell.

Logan swung himself out of his car and took the stairs two at a time. Then he pushed the rough, unpainted door open. Hard rock music slammed him. Just as he was about to step inside, the meaty claw of a biker's fist shot toward him through thick waves of cigarette smoke.

"Not so fast," Tommy snarled.

Logan smiled. "Hello, Tommy. Is Cici around?"

"What's it to you if she is?" he bellowed. "What in the devil makes you think you've got the right to set foot in here, Claiborne?"

Logan stared into the bloodshot blue eyes of T-Bos's bouncer. A dozen members of Tommy's little gang, all squatting around their dirty tables or leaning against the bar slammed their longnecks down and scowled at him.

Not that Logan recognized any of the hulking figures through the haze of smoke. Except for the neon beer signs, strings of colored lights decorating the bar, television sets mounted in every corner of the building and the flickering strobe lights, T-Bos's Bar was dimly lit. This was probably a good thing.

"Where's Cici?" Logan repeated.

Two bikers kicked their chairs over and stood up, stretching their brawny arms before crossing them menacingly over their wide chests and beer bellies.

"What business you got with Bos's Cici?" Tommy demanded.

"I called Bos, and Bos told me she was here."

"You talked to Bos?" Tommy relaxed visibly.

"He sent me."

"He damn sure didn't tell me."

"So call him, why don't you? Ask him."

"Bos don't like me botherin' him when he don't feel good, that's why."

When cockfighting had been legal, Logan's grandfather had pressured T-Bos to close his bar and his cockfighting establishment. Ever since the pit had been closed by new legislation, the Claibornes hadn't been the most popular people with Bos and his biker clientele.

"Cici's out back," Tommy finally said through gritted, yellow teeth. "You better not be lying about Bos sending you." Then with a meaningful shrug, Tommy disappeared. As his biker buddies crashed back in their chairs, even as their gazes pinned him, Logan heard him yelling for Cici.

A new song began to play that was even louder than the one before. Strobe lights began flashing to its beat.

In less than a minute Cici waltzed in looking like an angel in a pretty blue dress, the like of which Logan had never seen her wear before. Ablaze in the white light, she held a tray of glittering amber beer bottles high over her head.

Logan shoved a chair aside and loped through the throng of angry bikers to her. He felt embarrassed, nervous with so many tense gazes tracking him. When her shining eyes fixed on his face, she lowered her tray.

"You're crazy…coming here," she said. "Tommy's not too crazy about you."

"I had to see you. It doesn't make sense, but there it is. *I had to see you.* Ever since you came back, nothing in my life makes sense anymore."

She smiled, but tentatively. "You—being here—makes zero sense."

"I missed you today," he said.

"You said that on the phone. Why should I believe you?"

Her smile softened her expression, and something in her eyes welcomed him at least a little. Did she look dazzled? Or was it just the strobe lights? Well, a man could hope, couldn't he...maybe, just maybe it was him that had made her face go so soft and radiant.

Desire for her and some other emotion raced along his veins, lighting his nerves. The bikers' sharp gazes were drilling holes in his back. He should have been embarrassed or maybe scared to death. But suddenly he didn't care what any of them thought.

He caught her hand, pulled her nearer. It was simply too good to see her again after the long hours apart. Everything else he'd done today, Mitchell, Hayes, Alicia, the merger, Jake, seemed so unimportant. Which was crazy.

Although it was dark, he could detect her cheeks flush just as he felt himself washed with similar heat. Gently, he intertwined his fingers with hers and brought her hand to his lips. Then he gripped her fingers tightly and just held them against his cheek for a minute or two. It felt good, and so damn right, just to be with her.

"When do you get off work?" he asked finally, letting her go.

"Two hours."

"What can I do to help? I can wash glasses. Wait tables."

"No. You're to stay away from these guys. Pull up a stool behind the bar and just stay out of trouble. No conversation. Don't even look their way."

"You're letting me off too easy."

"If we get out of here without you getting into a fight, I'm happy. You're not too popular around here, you know."

"As long as you're glad I'm here…."

"I'm not making you any promises, Claiborne."

"Fair enough," he said.

When Cici left the bar on Logan's hard arm, her heart beat thunderously at the base of her neck.

"What do you want to do now?" she asked when they stood before their cars.

"First we kiss. Just once."

"Here? No way. We need to beat it."

"Here," he whispered sharply.

His tanned face lowered toward hers. His blue eyes flamed. Then his mouth touched hers as tenderly and innocently as he'd kissed her that first time, so many years ago when he'd made her realize it was him she wanted, not Jake. His body barely brushed hers. Even so, she felt his heat and wanted more.

Afterward, when he pulled away, he gazed down at her for a long moment. "Can we go somewhere and talk?" he asked.

It was harder for her to concentrate after his kiss. He was standing so close, and he felt so deliciously warm. Yet she couldn't let herself trust him.

"We could drive to Belle Rose. Make a pot of coffee and then drive into New Orleans," he said.

"Look, it's been a long day. I'll bet you're every bit as tired as I am. I think you should spend the night at Belle Rose. Not with me. In the big house across the hall from your grandfather. You should have breakfast with him. Pay attention to him."

"Okay, if I follow you home tonight, so I can make sure you don't have a breakdown?" he said.

She nodded. "I suppose that's allowed."

He opened her car door for her, and she slid inside.

"I'm glad you came tonight. I wanted to see you again. You know me—the wild swamp girl with the self-destructive streak."

"Cici, I want it to be different this time."

"I'm not sure I want…a this time," she replied. "I'm not sure I could ever trust you again."

"I don't blame you for feeling that way. All I can say is that ever since last night… I'm not myself."

"Right, you lost the merger and your girlfriend. So, you're feeling a little vulnerable."

He was about to argue, but she pressed a fingertip against his warm lips. "Cheer up. This too shall pass. You'll be your old killer, ambitious self in no time. I promise."

"Maybe that's not enough for me anymore."

"One night of sex with me and you're a changed man? Forgive me if I can't quite buy into the new, reformed Logan Claiborne. I know I'm good, but that would take a miracle worker." With a laugh she turned her key in the ignition and revved her engine. "Better hop in your car. You're going to have to drive pretty fast to catch me."

As she roared out of the parking lot, the last thing she saw was his headlights flash on and leap forward through the darkness after her.

The scent of freshly brewed coffee and cooked toast filled the high-ceilinged kitchen that had been used as the prep room in the olden days. Back then the large brick ovens in the real kitchen had been outside.

Through the open double doors, Cici could see the lovely dining room as she leaned against a long table, munching toast and sipping coffee. And for a moment, the room with its glittering crystal and silver seemed as fantastic as it had when she'd been a child, standing outside peering through the windows.

"Belle Rose was always a magical place to me," she said. "I used to love helping Noonoon cook. But most of all I loved hearing her stories about you and Jake."

"You were so infatuated with Jake back then."

"I did have a crush on him for years and years. He was so reckless and wild. Always doing something like chasing gators to get a girl's attention. You were so serious."

"You mean dull."

"No."

"Yes. I was dull because Grandpère was always throwing my father and mother up to me. Besides, one twin had to pay attention to business. I was ten minutes older and, therefore, the older, more responsible brother."

She laughed.

He opened the refrigerator. "There's leftover crawfish étouffée, dirty rice, yams and some gumbo. Are you hungry for more than toast?"

"I'm okay."

"It was wrong of me to come between you and Jake that last summer," he murmured, his voice growing darker as he shut the door. "Wrong to justify my actions by saying I was saving Jake from you. Wrong to give in to my grandfather's grudge against you."

"Are you finally apologizing?"

"For what it's worth, yes. But saying I'm sorry can't undo the past."

"You're right about that. But we wouldn't be here now, if you hadn't wooed me then." She faltered, not wanting to say more.

"And we wouldn't have had last night," he said.

"What are you saying?"

"I'm saying I'm not sorry about last night."

"Not even if it cost you the merger…and Alicia?"

"No. I'm not sorry."

She took a deep breath. "That's saying a lot, then."

"But do you believe me?"

"It's too early to tell. But I'll keep you posted."

"Cici…"

"What?"

"Nothing. Eat your toast."

He flushed darkly as if he suddenly felt shy around her.

She laughed. "Tongue-tied?"

"What's with the new, subdued look?" he asked. "The hair…brushed and tied back so neatly? The demure dress?"

"Maybe last night changed me, too. Although not as profoundly as you claim to be changed. But I'll be honest enough to admit that I was thinking about you when I bought this dress, thinking maybe I should try to tone my image down."

"Cici, I'm not asking you to change. You can even go with the Princess Leia look if you wish."

"Who said I was changing just to please you?"

"Nobody, but I do like the dress. Not that it matters."

Smiling, she set her empty coffee cup in the sink. "I guess I'll go out to the *garçonnière* now. Catch up on my beauty rest…"

"Would you like to go dancing first?" he asked. "Maybe at Rousseau's. That's not so far. And we wouldn't have to stay long."

He was smiling, and his eyes were sparkling. She was tired; she should be wary. But being wary was not in her nature.

"Maybe I wouldn't mind a little dancing," she said archly. "But only if we go in my car…and you let me drive…with the top down."

"I like a woman who likes to be in charge once in a while," he whispered.

"Well, don't you dare try to be a backseat driver."

His white teeth flashed as he put his arm around her and led her outside onto the gallery and then down to her Miata. Then he stopped and quickly wrote his grandfather a note telling him he'd found Cici and that they were driving to the well-known dance hall. After placing the note in the kitchen, they raced out to her car.

She put the top down and said, "Buckle your seat belt."

Once behind the wheel, she drove fast, maybe to scare him a little or maybe because that's the way she always drove. Not that he acted the least bit scared.

As the humid darkness flew by, he talked about how for years his life had been nothing but business. He told her that running Claiborne Energy was so challenging he often worked seventy-hour weeks, sometimes even more.

"I guess I thought I had to work like that because my father let Grandpère down, and maybe because Jake had walked out because of me. I think I thought I had a lot to make up for."

"Or maybe you were simply ambitious."

"Maybe."

Petrochemical plants along the river lit up the darkness from time to time, their smokestacks belching noxious fumes, but other stretches beside the levee were edged thickly with trees. They rushed past a stand of willows that streamed eerily in the breeze.

The moon was high and golden, but she paid it no attention. She was too busy watching the road and listening to him. When she saw the sign for Rousseau's, the wildly popular dance hall since the 1930s that was located on a tiny piece of sinking land beside the bayou, she pulled over.

"You were married," she said, after they found a picnic table on the plywood porch outside the dance hall, because his marriage interested her more than his work did. "Surely, even someone as ambitious as you didn't work all the time."

"But I did. I was never home."

"I'm sure she understood," Cici lied, hoping for more as she nibbled a cracker and watched a pair of elderly dancers through the windows as they slowly glided past them.

When Logan ordered beer and crawfish tails and andouille, a spicy, smoked sausage, she wondered how a man could eat so much and remain in such good shape.

"I guess I told myself she did…at the time," he said.

"I have to confess I've read about you and Noelle through the years. I poured over every glossy picture of you and her in front of your Italianate mansion in the Garden District I could find. Even when I was overseas I kept up on the Internet. I was still curious to know how the glamorous Claibornes lived. About how you lived."

"Magazine articles are as airbrushed as those photographs on their covers. They leave out a lot."

"Your life with Noelle sounded like a fairy tale," she said, turning the conversation back to what she was curious about.

"Yes. It was supposed to. We were much admired."

His deep voice sounded full of pain. "Image was important to me then."

"But no longer—after last night in my bed," she said.

"I think you've made that point before." His eyes met hers. "Don't sell yourself short. "Still, I've always had a knack for getting what I want, and back then, I was greedy for success." He hesitated. "But, be careful what you wish for, as they say. Even success can be dangerous."

She could tell him a thing or two about danger. Like tonight. What was she doing here with him? Listening to him? Believing him? Almost forgiving him?

She shifted on her seat. "So why did you come looking for me tonight?"

"You mean besides the fact that you are a sexual goddess."

She laughed.

"You are, you know?"

"Right."

"You're spectacular. And not just in bed." His hand reached across the table and folded hers inside his fingers, causing a trill of warm sensation to flood her.

"Cici, I received many calls today, thanking me for the wonderful party I threw my grandfather. Apparently, he had the time of his life all because of you. Thank you for making him so happy."

"I can't take all the credit. You paid for everything. You've been letting him come into the office."

"You showed me that I was neglecting him…just like I neglected Noelle. And he's actually proved himself useful at the office. He knows so much about the company's past, and he's very wise. Hopefully, because of you, I'll be more attentive to him in the future."

"Like having breakfast with him in the morning?"

"Like that."

She smiled. "He loves you so much."

"I love him, too. I owe him everything."

"Funny, how easy it is to forget those we love sometimes."

"Not so funny." He pressed her hand tightly and then brought it to his lips. He kissed her fingertips warmly. "I've run roughshod over the people I've loved," he whispered. "It's time I stopped."

"You know what they say about good intentions, Claiborne."

"If you can wear that demure blue dress, maybe I can change a feather or two of my plumage."

"It's not so easy, you know."

"You forget how determined I can be when I want something."

Their food and beer came, and he withdrew his hand. She ordered more crackers. For a while their food and drink proved so distracting, they didn't talk. Then he asked her to dance, and being held in his arms was even more distracting than chatting or holding hands or eating had been.

He pulled her close, his voice in her ear as they swirled faster than the elderly dancers. Tonight there was no one to stop them from dancing with each other as long as they liked, so they remained on the dance floor for nearly an hour. She was breathless when he led her back to their table.

"It's late, and I'm very tired," she said. "Would you drive me home?"

"You trust me to drive?"

"Yes, but that's all I trust you to do."

"For now," he said in a husky tone.

Nine

It was a balmy spring morning with water splashing in the nearby fountain and bees buzzing in the azalea blossoms.

Logan was being the perfect gentleman, not that he was to be trusted, Cici reminded herself. Still, she was enjoying his company as well as Pierre's way more than she wanted to as she sipped steaming chicory coffee and nibbled at her scrambled eggs and spicy Chaurice sausage on the wide veranda.

A swamp girl could get used to the high life. Yes, she felt totally at ease with them and their elegant surroundings as the old man proceeded to extract each detail concerning the failed merger from his grandson.

"This is a temporary setback," Pierre said. "A challenge. Mitchell will come around."

"I don't think so, and frankly…I'm not sure…" Logan's sudden grin revealed a flash of straight white teeth.

Underneath the tablecloth, his leg was nudging Cici's much too flirtatiously, causing her to gasp.

"You'll see. If you ask me, Mitchell was a bit too happy to sink the deal," Pierre murmured before turning to include Cici. "But we're boring you."

The warm heat of Logan's calf grazing hers had her blushing now.

"Not at all," she murmured, scooting further away from Logan.

Pierre patted her hand. "Nevertheless, I insist we talk about the wonderful party you gave me. I had the time of my life—seeing friends I hadn't seen in months."

"I'm glad," she said.

"Me, too," Logan agreed.

When breakfast was over, Logan walked her to the library before he had to leave for the city.

"You make him happy," he said. "I like that. Still, I'd like to be selfish and borrow you so I could enjoy you myself for a while. I do have a library in New Orleans, every bit as good as this one."

"I'd love to see it sometime," she murmured carelessly as she lifted a book off a table.

Gently he took the book from her and closed it. Setting it down, he said, "Why not today? Cici, I think we've wasted enough time…and all because I was such a fool."

"You were far worse than that."

"You're right. And I am sorry. And I know I'm probably rushing you, but like I said, I'm selfish. I'd really like for you to follow me back this morning. I lay awake all night thinking about this. We need to get to know each other better."

"I grew up here, remember. I've known you most of my life."

"I mean…know each other as adults. I have a huge house. You could stay in it…write in my library. I'd be away all day, but in the evening we could go out together. We could talk, dance… We could see where this thing between us is going."

"I don't think so. My uncle is here. I'm set up here…"

"Why not? Just for a day or two, then. What if I promise not to touch you?"

"That would be dull indeed."

"Don't tease me. What I'm suggesting is an old-fashioned courtship."

"Forgive me if I'm missing something, but I don't think old-fashioned courtships have ever consisted of young women who've already spent the night in a young man's arms moving in with him."

"Well, then it'll be an old-fashioned courtship with a modern twist. What do you say, Cici?"

"You probably think this is just the sort of proposition that would appeal to a swamp girl like me."

"I beg you not to tease me."

"That's harder than you think, you know."

"Will you come?"

"I shouldn't."

It was nearly noon when Cici followed Logan's Lexus up his narrow driveway in the Garden District. Looking up, she saw his double-galleried, three-story, Italianate mansion lit softly by golden sunshine filtering through the trees.

Grinning at her for gaping at his mansion, he got out of his Lexus and swung her car door open. "Well, what do you think?"

"Your city home is every bit as impressive and magical as Belle Rose."

"I hoped you'd like it. And, remember, I'm not bringing you here for sex."

"Oh, really?" she teased, lifting her eyebrows with a pretense of schoolteacher primness. "But would a man who clearly wants to impress a girl with his wealth turn it down if *she* offered it?"

"Such a girl shouldn't push her luck. Not with a man whose character has been less than perfect in the past. There are six bedrooms in this house. You can have any of them."

"Even yours?"

"That one, too. I repeat: your choice. But I thought maybe we should slow it down."

"What a shame." With a smile she followed him up the stairs onto the lower gallery of his fabulous mansion.

After a night of passion, he had come after her, saying he was a changed man. He had brought her here to his home, saying he wanted to formally court her. Nonsense...probably...even thought he did seem boyishly sincere.

His mansion was as formal and classical inside as the outside.

"Oh, how lovely it all is, but then I knew it would be," she said. "But then I already said that, didn't I?"

"My mother restored this home as well as Belle Rose. She had impeccable taste and spared no expense. It would have been a marvel simply to restore both houses, but, no, leave it to her to acquire original furniture, portraits, and then mix them with antiques she carefully chose."

"So, do you have time to give me a tour of this wonderful house before you go to the office?"

"All right. For starters, the house was built in 1860, right before the Civil War. I'm sure Noonoon told you that our family were royals who left France with nothing but the clothes on their backs and their jewels sewed into their pockets during the French revolution. Because of their title, their children married into the wealthier families in Louisiana. So, marrying well has always been part of the family culture."

"No wonder your grandfather didn't want a girl like me for one of his grandsons," Cici said.

"Times change. But back then our ambitious family

bought plantations with their jewels. By marrying well, too, they prospered. Then one of my most enchanting Creole ancestors, Francoise, married Able Claiborne, an extremely rich American, and he gave her this house for a wedding present."

"Lucky girl."

"What if I told you he kept the quadroon mistress he'd been in love with before his marriage?"

"Right. Back then a man could marry well and maintain the woman he really loved on the side."

"Sometimes. In any case, Francoise didn't get to enjoy her honeymoon here long. The Yankees occupied the house during the war. When she got it back, she was horrified to find her furniture burned for firewood and hoof prints from the Yankees' horses on the ballroom floor and stairs. Of course, now these very same hoof prints are much prized."

Cici laughed. "And I thought that was a cliché."

"It is."

He led her to the staircase and showed her the hoof marks. Then she looked up as he explained that the staircase coiled upward past large windows and double doors that opened onto a back piazza. The ceiling above the graceful stairs had magnificent plasterwork and a stained glass oculus in its center.

Once upstairs, he showed her all six bedrooms, the last and most splendid being his large master bedroom where an immense four-poster bed dwarfed the other furnishings.

"So, which bed will you choose as yours?" he asked, catching her off guard while she stared at his red satin spread.

Startled, she whirled. In the confined space of his bedroom, his height and wide shoulders made him seem huge. Or was it his teasing reckless grin that made her feel so vulnerable?

"Why…why…maybe that last one at the end of the hall," she said too quickly.

"The one that is as far from mine as possible?"

"Exactly! You did say you wanted an old-fashioned courtship."

His grin broadened.

She caught her breath.

"Relax. I'll bring your bags up before I go to the office. The kitchen downstairs is well stocked. If you need anything you can't find, anything at all, don't hesitate to call me." He pulled out a business card that contained all his phone numbers and circled his cell number. Then he leaned down and planted a chaste kiss on her cheek.

"You didn't show me the library," she whispered even as her heart drummed violently in reaction to his lips.

"Oh, that," he said, his breath warm against her skin.

"After all, it was your library that tempted me to accept your invitation."

"Not me?"

"No, definitely, it was your library."

"I warned you about teasing me," he murmured in a

husky undertone. "Now I really must prove you wrong."
He caught her hand and pulled her nearer.

"What are you doing?"

"Taking you up on your challenge." Catching her
shoulders he pulled her into his arms. She let out a little
cry before his mouth came down on hers.

His kiss was so tenderly reverent, she imagined in
its sweet heat promises he'd never made before, promises
she didn't dare let herself believe. And suddenly all the
joy she'd hoped to find in his loving her when she'd
been a naive eighteen-year-old girl filled her heart anew,
and she surrendered to his exploring tongue for a few
delicious moments without the slightest reservation.

Her arms came around his neck, and she clung with
far too much relish. But slowly sanity returned and she
remembered that a woman her age had to be smart about
wealthy, sophisticated men like him. Sucking in a sharp
breath, she pushed against his chest.

Reluctantly he released her. "I'll get your bags."
Then he turned, and she heard his footsteps loping
down the stairs.

In his beautiful bedroom, she stared after him and
longed for another taste of him, longed for all the things
that had been rudely ripped from her when she was
eight…and then ripped from her again by him
later…love…security…family…the sense of belonging to someone, somewhere, forever.

Before she knew it, she heard him downstairs again,
returning with her bags. The last thing she needed was for

him to discover her in his bedroom so shaken from his kiss she was harboring all sorts of wildly romantic fantasies.

Determined to get to work and get her mind off him, she dashed down the stairs to explore his library while he carried her luggage up to her room.

Knowing that Cici was at his house and would be waiting for him, made it more difficult for Logan to concentrate than usual. He called her twice. When she said he was interrupting her, he called her back and then teased her for answering when she chided him again.

He hung up. Almost immediately he picked up the phone and called a florist to order flowers for her.

Five minutes later he was on the verge of calling her back when Hayes strode inside his office without knocking.

"Good news," Hayes said, his black eyes as sharp as his voice. "At least, it could be good for us. There's rather more to Mitchell Butler's asbestos problem than he led us to believe. Not only that, he's just lost that big government contract to build more patrol boats for the U.S. Coast Guard. He's carrying a boatload of foreign debt. I think he's in trouble with the Feds."

Hayes went to Logan's computer and pulled up a Web page.

"Wow, this is bad," Logan said. "He's been bilking the company like a bandit. Looks like you need to give him a call and make a new offer."

"What exactly do you have in mind?"

When Logan gave him a rock bottom number, Hayes let out a low whistle. "You certainly haven't lost your killer instinct. Yesterday you were so down…"

"Save the compliments. Just make the offer. See what he says. Then get back to me."

"Enjoying your crispy quail salad?" Logan said.

"Oh, my goodness, yes!" Setting her fork down, Cici glanced up at him. "Excuse me. Yes." She dabbed her lip with her napkin. "It's delicious."

"So delicious, you haven't said a word to me in at least five minutes. I never thought I'd be jealous of a quail salad."

She laughed. "Then order one for yourself."

"Did you get anything done on your book?"

"Your library was too fantastic. You might say I bogged down in my research."

Their restaurant was located in the heart of the French Quarter. He'd told her it was world famous, and she could see why. It's soft lighting, slow but attentive service and excellent food made for the most romantic dining experience, at least, when a girl wasn't gorging on her quail salad.

"I didn't mean for you to stop eating," he said. Then he frowned as he glanced to his right at a couple who'd just walked in and were being seated at a table against the far wall.

"Oh, no," he murmured when the brunette, who'd

been about to take her chair, saw him, stood up again and fled.

"Alicia?" Cici hadn't seen much of the woman other than her stricken expression and slim back, so she wasn't sure who it was.

"I'm afraid so."

Her companion, an older man with a tanned face and thick, silver hair, stood up and turned toward Logan. Instead of following his dinner companion, the man threw down his napkin and strode over to their table. When Logan thrust out his hand, the man stared at it so coldly, Logan let it fall to his side.

"Your CEO called me today, Claiborne."

"Sorry to hear about your recent…er…troubles," Logan said. "Still, you weren't completely honest."

"So, you're moving in for the kill." Mitchell's expression darkened as he turned vengefully to Cici. "I'd watch him, if I were you, young lady. He's not just some nice, tame guy who takes pretty girls to expensive restaurants. He eats people alive."

"That's uncalled for, Butler."

"Is it?"

"You were the one who lied. I'm merely exposing the lie and offering to bail you out." Logan pushed his chair back, but not before Mitchell had begun backing away from the table.

"Go to hell."

"If you're smart, you'll consider my offer." Logan turned back to Cici. "Sorry about that," he added. "I hope he didn't ruin your quail salad. He and I have some unfinished business. I'm afraid he wasn't entirely forthcoming about his shipyard. Or his other affairs."

"Nothing could spoil my salad," she whispered.

But strangely, as it turned out, she couldn't eat another bite. She kept remembering Alicia's stricken look and Mitchell's warning to her about Logan. Of course, the man was bitter about the merger and Logan's new offer, so his words could mean nothing. Still, it was nearly half an hour before she could resume her participation in the light banter they'd been enjoying before Mitchell Butler had so rudely interrupted them.

Who better than she should know that Logan was not a nice, tame guy?

He eats people alive.

Was that true? If so, did that still include the people he loved?

Ten

In silence Logan walked Cici up the stairs and down to her bedroom where they stood together in the long shadows sweeping the hall, holding hands.

"I'm sorry about Mitchell," Logan repeated, pressing her fingers.

She licked her lips. "You wanted me to come here so we could get to know one another better. You're a business man, and he's part of your world. Maybe it's for the best that I met him and realized some people see you as a hard, ambitious businessman."

"Maybe. But I would have preferred different circumstances for our first night out together."

"And what would they have been?"

"I was dining with you. I didn't feel like being sur-prised, at least, not by Mitchell. He's not a particularly nice guy." He paused. "Well, I guess I'll say good night."

When he leaned down to kiss her, she stood on her tiptoes, eager for his lips, surrendering the instant his mouth claimed hers. She wanted more than a good-night kiss. Yes, what she wanted was to acquiesce to the passion she felt for him again, as she had that night in the *garçonnière*.

Still, she couldn't let herself fall under his spell. If it didn't work out, she would be getting in too deep, too fast again. He was right about the need to slow it down.

"It feels warm all of a sudden," he said.

Because of his kisses, heat blazed through her, too, and made her tremble.

He undid the ribbon in her hair, so that untidy masses of springy gold flowed silkily over her shoulders. A shiver rippled through her. Feeling herself on the brink of surrender, she caught her breath. Then, making a huge effort to behave wisely and heed Mitchell Butler's warning, she clenched her hands against her sides, and determined to fight the awaken-ing desires in her body.

Their night together in the *garçonnière* had made her know too well, exactly how much she wanted him. When he hadn't called all day, she'd felt rejected all over again. How much trust could she place in him?

Reading her transparent face, he sighed and took a

long step backward. "Maybe Mitchell's right. Maybe you should doubt me," he said.

An acute feeling of empathy swept her. "I hope not."

"Sleep well, Cici. You'll find everything you need in your bedroom. Oversized T-shirts or regular nightgowns to sleep in…whatever you prefer…a new toothbrush. The bathroom's in the corner…"

"I know. You're very generous."

"I wouldn't argue that point with Mitchell."

She didn't smile at his attempt at humor.

She longed for another kiss, longed for it so much she feared it. Determined to be strong, she turned away, walked inside her room and shut her door.

As if a piece of wood between them could make her heart stop racing or her blood cool. She closed her eyes and leaned against the thick door for many minutes, counting backward from one hundred until she felt calmer. When she reached the number twenty, she padded over to the bed and pulled back the heavy covers, determining that tonight, as he'd promised, they would sleep apart.

Choosing a scarlet nightgown instead of a long white T-shirt, Cici showered and dressed for bed in Logan's perfectly-appointed, pink marble guest bathroom. As she slipped the cool, red silk gown over her shoulders and let it slide down her body, Cici couldn't help but wonder how many women Logan had brought here before her.

Turning away from the mirror she returned to her

bedroom. Had Alicia slept in this same room? Worn this nightgown?

Probably not. Feeling cherished, Alicia had no doubt lain naked in Logan's arms in the master bedroom.

Frowning, not wanting to dwell on Alicia, who'd run at the sight of Logan tonight, Cici climbed into her bed and squeezed her eyes shut.

No matter what Mitchell had said, she was here tonight, tucked between Logan's crisp, sweet-smelling sheets. He'd been sweet to her, attentive, protective even. He'd said he wanted to be with her. And not just for sex. But was he trustworthy?

Wanting desperately to believe him, she shut off her light. But the darkness made her feel strange and lonely in Logan's big, unfamiliar guest bed, and she couldn't stop thinking about him being at the end of the hall in his own big red bed. At the thought of his long, tanned body beneath his equally crisp sheets, the pulse in her throat began to jump erratically. Her skin started to burn, and soon she was so hot she threw off her covers. Was he as wide-awake as she was?

Slowly she arose from her bed. Stretching and then sighing, she walked restlessly to the door inside her bedroom that opened out onto the gallery. Stars lit the black sky. Maybe fresh air would make her relax and feel sleepy.

Pulling the drapes back and unlocking the door, she would have stepped outside, but a four-alarm siren began to scream through the house.

Putting her hands over her ears, she swallowed. She'd probably awakened everybody in the neighborhood. Not to mention, Logan.

In the next minute, the siren stopped, and Logan began knocking loudly on her hall door.

"Come in."

He stepped inside, holding a cordless phone. Clad only in a pair of black pajama bottoms, her heart sped up at the sight of his wide, dusky shoulders and cut abdomen.

"Are you all right?" he asked.

"I couldn't sleep," she said. "I'm sorry."

The phone rang, and he told his security company that a guest had opened a door but that everything was fine. He gave them his code and hung up.

"You can open your door now," he said. "I should have told you about the alarm. This is New Orleans. Our crime rate is not the best in the country."

"I know that, of course. I should have thought. But then since I camped out in so many war zones, I probably don't worry about crime the same way normal people do…even in New Orleans."

"Don't remind me of how you lived…because of my actions."

"Don't blame yourself entirely. I was an adult."

"You were a young, vulnerable woman, whose heart was broken."

"Don't…"

He said no more on the subject. When she stepped outside onto the gallery, he joined her. She slid into the moonlight while he kept in the deep shadows, his feral eyes gleaming in the dark as he watched her every movement.

"I couldn't sleep…for thinking about you," she admitted, her gaze drifting over his muscular brown chest and hard arms again.

A light breeze caused her silk gown to ripple and cling to her swollen nipples as well as to the lush curves of her hips and legs.

"Funny, I'm having the same problem," he said, his deep voice husky. "I shouldn't have followed you out here."

Her senses catapulted in alarm. Sexual chemistry seemed to ignite the air between them. To hide her nervousness she slid her hand back and forth along the slick black railing and laughed softly. "I forget. Why exactly are we sleeping apart tonight?"

"Old-fashioned courtship. So that I can prove I don't want you just for sex."

"Oh, right." *So, why were his warm, gleaming eyes glued so hungrily to her breasts?*

"Now we know why old-fashioned courtships didn't sanction sleepovers," she said. "Hey, maybe I've always been too open to risk. Maybe I don't have to know you're perfect and will treat me perfectly forever and ever."

"You're sure about that when I still don't know how I see this thing between us long-term," he said.

"Maybe I want to lie cuddled in your arms all night too much to resist sharing your bed."

He sighed. "I wouldn't say no. But then, be honest.

Ask yourself, once you're in my bed, do you really think you can trust me to stop at cuddling."

"Or me? I just said cuddling to make myself sound ladylike…and…er…demure."

His gaze seared her. Even though she felt his swift movement toward her through the darkness, she hissed in a breath when his big hands wrapped her close, his heat instantly warming every sensual cell in her body.

Fool. Fool.

She couldn't help herself. She felt small and feminine and very desirable in his arms. Like a marshmallow over a fire, she burned on the outside and turned to mush on the inside.

His lips eager, he kissed her brow, her mouth. When he finally let her go, her heart was thudding furiously in her throat, and her entire being was ablaze.

"Cici, I don't know what I felt nine years ago, but whatever it was, it damn sure knocked me off course. I'd been dating Noelle when I came down to Belle Rose to see Grandpère and Jake that summer. I'd even decided to marry her. Not that I'd asked her or that I was even seeing her exclusively. Still, I'd made up my mind."

"You were good at that. Stubborn to the core once you set your course."

"So, when I saw you in your pirogue that first day and realized you were all grown up, I never imagined that you and I could ever be seriously involved…even after Grandpère convinced me I had to save Jake from you." He broke off.

"I understand. There was no place for me in your life."

"I was slightly angry that you weren't that cute little bratty girl who followed me around in the swamp anymore, but there you were with the sunlight in your hair. A sex goddess of the swamp. Irresistible."

"Little girls do have a way of growing up."

"Yes. Do they ever. I couldn't take my eyes off you. When Grandpère convinced me to save Jake, I soon became so obsessed with you myself, I no longer knew what I was doing. Not that I could admit it."

Logan bent his head and kissed her softly. "After we made love, I was wild to have you again. And again. Then you told me you were in love with me, and I realized maybe I'd gone too far."

"Because I was naive."

"I…I was so determined to go out and conquer the world. My grandfather was convinced I had to have someone like Noelle at my side. He had my life all planned out. Since the family was in trouble, I went along with whatever he said. I didn't think I had the freedom to choose."

"And you had Noelle waiting in the wings."

"I was stupid where she was concerned. She was never more than an illusion. I should have behaved more responsibly toward both of you."

Logan was caressing her with both hands, slowly running his callused fingers down her arms and hips, causing her to shiver.

"Do we have to rehash all this…when it feel so good just to be together?"

"I want you to know how it was with me…and Noelle. I married her on the rebound. I was still crazy about you. Maybe I told myself in the beginning that I seduced you to keep Jake from having you, but that couldn't have been all there was to it. Because of my feelings for you, I was messed up for years, maybe until I saw you naked in the *garçonnière* and wanted you so fiercely. I never felt a tenth for her what I felt for you that day. I sure as hell never loved her. Looking back I see that I worked all the time, probably to avoid being home alone with her and having to face the truth. As I told you before, I'm afraid I neglected her and made her very unhappy. She told me how miserable I'd made her shortly before she died. She tried so hard to be a good wife, too. She was a lovely woman. She didn't deserve to be slighted any more than you did. I'll always regret how I treated her. Not that it fixes anything. She's dead. There's no going back."

"Why are you telling me all this?"

"Who knows? As a little girl, you looked at our big house and at us, and you built the Claibornes up into lordly beings we aren't."

"Like my book title, *Lords of the Bayou*."

"Exactly. I want you to know who we are, at least, who I am, warts and all. I don't want to lead you on."

"Don't worry. How could I have illusions about you after how you treated me? But you thought you were doing what was best for your family. It's in the past."

"I was blind."

"So was I."

"I'm so sorry."

Then she pressed a single fingertip against his mouth. "I don't care about the past," she whispered.

Logan began to caress her with both hands, causing her to shiver.

"You're so soft and feminine," he said. "So beautiful. So sweet. How could I have ever thought you couldn't suit me?"

"Maybe because you were too used to thinking of me as a child who was constantly out to get your attention by doing all those silly things…like stealing your hat or hiding your fishing lures."

"Back then you were a part of my life, like the air I breathed. I took you for granted."

And now? What did he feel now? She pulled free of his embrace and ran the length of the hall to his bedroom, knowing he would follow. Maybe she shouldn't make love to him with so many unanswered questions, but she couldn't seem to stop herself.

"From the moment I heard you'd come back to Belle Rose, I've been like a man possessed."

Something inside her she'd thought long dead had instantly taken her over from the moment she'd seen him at the *garçonnière*. Ever since she'd made love to him, she'd been consumed by her feelings for him. She wanted him. And not just for a casual affair. He felt essential in ways she couldn't fathom.

Inside his bedroom, she whispered a single word. "Condom?"

"Right," he muttered, his own voice as rough as hers. "Almost forgot."

After he led her to the bed, she was vaguely aware of him opening a drawer and shredding a foil wrapper. Then he was like a man possessed as he kissed her lips and throat and breasts before savagely tearing off his clothes as she flung her own off onto the floor.

Sheathed, he pulled her under him on the bed. Then he lowered himself over her and drove himself inside her soft, wet depths with a single thrust. On a blissful sigh she locked her legs around his hips and held on tight. Not that he remained still long.

Suddenly there seemed no softness or tenderness in him. But she didn't care as he drove into her again and again. Tonight she wanted it fast and hard. She wanted to be claimed, possessed and dominated. No matter what the future held, she wanted to feel that she was his, solely his, if only for tonight.

Their mating was fierce and violent. It was almost as if they'd each been afraid she thought afterward as she lay trembling and spent in his hard, warm arms. But afraid of what? Surely not Butler's warning at dinner.

Logan made love to her again and again that night, and every time her hips surged to meet his, their bodies locked in the perfect rhythm of an ancient dance. Always as he slid inside her depths, into the hot sleek perfection of her womanhood, she would writhe and cling as her own pleasure engulfed her. But each time her excitement held that strange, desperate quality, even as it built past anything she had ever known.

When it was over, she knew she had to tell him about their son.

Eleven

"Logan?"

"What is it, darling?" he murmured drowsily.

She pulled free of his arms. At the thought of the little boy they'd lost, misery made her tremble. "You asked about my scar. It's from a Cesarean operation. The reason I called you in the fall after that summer we were lovers…was…was to tell you…that…that I, that I was pregnant…with your child."

His body went rigid. Then she felt him slide away from her, leaving her wrapped in coldness.

"Oh, my God… I never once thought of that," he muttered.

Her eyes filled with tears, so his shadowy form on

the other side of the bed became a merciful blur. "I know. And before I could…say anything you…"

"I cut you off by telling you that I'd married Noelle," he said in a low, dead voice. "Always the bastard…"

"No…"

"Damn it, yes! I am. I had to get you off the phone because just talking to you made me know how much I still wanted you. And I was married. Did I think of how I was hurting you? Did I?" Finally, he said, "Tell me everything."

"I was so devastated I didn't care if I lived or died," she admitted, her voice thick with remembered pain.

He was silent for a long time. When he finally spoke again, his low tone had a faraway quality. "How did you manage alone without my help?"

"I don't know." She lay back against her pillow and stared up at the dark ceiling. "Somehow I just got through the days, one at a time. I guess I took care of myself…because of our precious baby." She paused. "Even so, he only lived a day. That was the worst part."

"He?"

"We had a son. He had dark hair like yours. I loved him so much…more than anything. I named him Logan."

"Oh, my God! So, that's why you cried when I kissed your scar in the *garçonnière,* why you're crying now," he said, his voice still strange and distant. "He died, and you had to face all that alone. It must have been unbearable. I can't believe I was so horribly cold to you…even before the worst had happened."

"You didn't know."

"As if that excuses my behavior. What did you do next?"

"I buried our baby and my pain. I tried to forget him and you as well, by hiding behind my camera. For years, I preferred to be a witness to other people's pain."

"No wonder."

Something in his voice and manner filled her with new apprehension.

"Even though I was running from my own heartbreak, I wanted my pictures to scream victims' stories, maybe because my own pain was locked so tightly in my heart."

"You threw yourself in danger because of what I did to you and our son. You could have died, and I would never have known how deeply I had wronged you. I would never have known about our little boy. I would have gone on living my silly, stupid, self-serving life. Mitchell Butler is right about me."

He sounded so utterly stricken, she lifted her gaze to his and found his eyes cloudy with dark emotion.

"It wasn't *all* your fault," she said gently. "Maybe I should have been stronger. Or maybe I was too bold. I did sort of throw myself at you that summer."

"As many young girls do, who don't know the power of their sexuality and where it can lead. No, I was older. I should have faced the reality of what I did, of what happened…that I cared about you…*deeply.* I knew you loved me, and I was stupid and cruel and set on an idiotic course because of outdated ideas about duty and family. Damn." Guilt and shame filled his broken tone.

She leaned across the bed to touch him, to comfort him, but the moment her fingertips slid against the hot, hard flesh of his shoulder, he jerked away from her.

"No. I don't deserve you. Not after this."

"Logan, it was a long time ago."

"Do you think that matters?" he demanded icily. "I should have thought about the possibility of a baby. I should have listened when you called me. Cici, oh, God, Cici, I'll never forgive myself for making you go through that alone. I can't even begin to imagine how terrible it all must have been for you."

When he stood up and began to dress, her heart began to slam in slow, painful beats. "I didn't tell you about our son to make you unhappier or guiltier. I think I forgave you a long time ago. Tonight, I just wanted to share his short life and my love for him with you. That's all. I wanted you to know that we had this precious, darling son together."

"Well, I'm glad you told me," he said coldly. "Now I'm going out. I have to be alone."

"But Logan…I need you…"

"No, you don't. When have I ever satisfied any of your real needs? Tomorrow I think you should leave."

"What? You're sending me away?"

"It's for your own good."

"You're really serious?"

"Someday you'll thank me," he said savagely.

"No. I won't. Don't I have any rights in this relationship?"

"Like I said, you'll be better off!"

"But what if I don't see it that way? You have no right to make this decision for me."

"I have news for you. The decision has been made." He stalked toward the door.

"You're as high-handed and arrogant and hateful as you always were!" she shouted.

"Finally, you understand me as well as Mitchell Butler does—only he's got an advantage—because he's exactly like me. I eat people alive!" He opened the door, banged it shut and was gone.

She heard his footsteps slamming down the stairs. The front door opened and closed. She heard his car start. Then tires squealed down the drive.

After that, except for the pulse that knocked painfully in her throat, his empty house was silent and still.

Eight hours later the gray afternoon sky threatened rain as Logan knelt before Noelle's white marble, above-ground tomb in Lafayette Cemetery No. 1.

Carefully he laid a single red rose on the gleaming white step before the marble angel that bore a profound likeness to Noelle.

"I'm sorry I made you so unhappy," he whispered, hoping she could hear him. "I wanted to marry you so much. I was so sure I was doing the right thing. But I lied to you. And to myself. And I hurt you…just as much as I hurt Cici and our son. Just as much."

There was a low sigh, and he started. Looking up, he saw it was only the wind in the trees.

How could he have been so horribly wrong about everything when he'd been so sure he was right? He'd hurt so many people he'd thought he'd loved.

Last night when Cici had told him about their son, the pain in her voice had pierced his heart like a knife. If he'd helped her back then, maybe their son would be alive.

He'd driven around all morning, thinking about Cici and all that he'd put her through. He loved her, but after the torment he'd caused her, he knew he didn't deserve her.

He loved her. Maybe he'd always loved her. Too bad he hadn't known it until it was too late.

He had to let her go. For once in his life he wouldn't go after what he selfishly wanted, just because he wanted it.

He wasn't worthy of her. She was better off without him.

Slowly he arose, and as he walked out of the cemetery he thought of the bleak, empty years ahead and wondered how he would ever find the courage to face a future that didn't include Cici Bellefleur. Would he ever be able to live with what he'd done to her?

Cici was wearing dark glasses to hide her red eyes as she stepped out of the elevator on Logan's floor late that afternoon just as Mitchell Butler rushed from the offices of Claiborne Energy.

"You!" he snapped, bristling upon seeing her.

"Good afternoon," she whispered as she tried to move past him.

He grabbed her arm and then realizing he shouldn't have done so, dropped it. "If you're smart, young lady, you'll stay away from him. He's marrying my daughter, Alicia."

"What?"

"Don't say I didn't try to warn you last night. He's buying my shipyard and marrying my daughter—to seal the bargain, so to speak. So if you think he wants to have anything to do with you, you're crazy."

"If you think I'll take your word for that, Mr. Butler, you're the one who's crazy! I know you probably feel pretty desperate about the merger. You'd do or say anything…"

Hatred and wrath seemed to spew from his eyes even as his jaw went slack. Not wishing to prolong their unpleasant exchange, Cici ran past him into Mrs. Dilling's outer office.

"Is your boss here?" she asked, turning to see if Mr. Butler had followed her and feeling relieved when she saw he hadn't.

"Sorry," the woman said as she looked up from her computer.

"Where is he?"

"Do you have an appointment…Miss Bellefleur, is it?"

Cici nodded. "When…when do you expect him?"

"Not until next week. Do you wish to make an appointment?"

Without bothering to answer her, Cici walked to Logan's door and threw it open. Like his house, his office was empty and felt cold and dead without him in it.

"He'll be back next week," Mrs. Dillings said from behind her. "I'd be happy to schedule—"

"That won't be necessary," Cici said in a dull, defeated tone. "He's made it very clear he doesn't really want to see me."

The next morning an article in the *Times-Picayune* caused quite a stir over breakfast at Belle Rose as the early morning sun slanted across the emerald-green lawn and turned the columns of Belle Rose to pillars of gold.

"Mitchell Butler says right here that Claiborne Energy is buying Butler Shipyard and that Logan's marrying his daughter," Pierre said. "I thought you and he…I mean I thought that you went to New Orleans to be with Logan."

Cici didn't trust Butler, so she wasn't so sure that Mitchell's account was entirely accurate. Still, since what he said upset Pierre, her hands tensed as she tried to frame an answer.

"I'm afraid that's all over," she said. "I'm going on assignment to Egypt. A feature story about…"

"But you can't leave," Pierre said from his wicker chair on the gallery. "What about our tours? And your book? Our research? Our interviews? Logan?"

Wincing because he'd been so enthusiastic about helping her when she'd first arrived and now, because now at the thought of her leaving, he looked so small and lost, Cici gently set her tea cup down.

Leaning toward him, she patted his hand. Its coolness and thinness along with the slight tremor she detected frightened her a little.

"You know you can give the tours without me. And…my agent got that extension she promised me, so I can put the book off for a while."

"But I just set up an interview with Eugene Thibodeaux. And I told you how busy he is."

"I'm sorry, but I'm afraid I must ask you to cancel it."

"Because of Logan?"

"I do have a life of my own you know," she said.

Pierre's hands had begun to shake. The color had drained from his face. He looked too white, too thin, and very old.

Damn Mitchell Butler.

All lives, but especially those of the very young and the elderly are so fragile. Because of Butler, Pierre, who didn't need to be upset, was in real emotional pain.

"I'm truly sorry, Pierre," Cici said softly. "But I'm afraid this can't be helped."

Her uncle chose that moment to call her on her mobile and say he'd read the article.

"Not now," she whispered. "I'm trying to explain the situation to Pierre."

"As if anything needs explaining," he said. "Call me back when you get the chance." He hung up.

"It's my fault," Pierre said. "I was too imperious and intolerant back in the old days. And I insisted Logan follow suit. Together we've made you think you don't really belong and can never be happy here."

At the thought of losing the chance at happiness she'd longed for only yesterday, her voice caught. "You've made me happy while I've been here this time."

"Not happy enough apparently."

As he lifted his coffee cup, she wondered if Pierre had heard anything she'd said other than that she was leaving. His face was pinched and set, and he was squinting as he stared unseeingly into the sun in the direction of the swamp and her uncle's land beyond.

He'd adjust, just as she would. He just needed time. Anybody who'd lived as long as he had knew changes and losses were inevitable.

"I'll go and make an airplane reservation," she said.

He looked so ashen and lost as she arose, she wondered if she should call Logan and warn him she was worried about him. After all, he'd give her all his phone numbers.

No, he'd made it clear he couldn't deal with the past or his guilt or her.

She wouldn't talk to him; she would tell Noonoon to call him instead.

Twelve

Logan's bedroom television was blaring. Not that he was concentrating on it even though the story was about Mitchell's deluded lies. The man's empire was built on hype and debt. He'd gone off his rocker after Hayes had pitched Mitchell his offer.

Not that Logan was thinking about Mitchell. He'd asked Hayes to deal with Mitchell.

All Logan could think of was Cici. Did she believe Mitchell about Alicia? If she did, maybe it was for the best. She would hate him more and forget him sooner.

Logan's gaze drifted to his bed. In this room, on that bed, he'd made love to her for the last time, a mere twenty-four hours ago. He'd been the happiest man in the world until she'd told him about their son and he'd realized how utterly unforgivable his behavior to her had been. In some ways he was exactly like Mitchell Butler.

Noonoon had told Logan Cici would be leaving for Egypt soon. He regretted driving her away, and it saddened him he might not see her again for years. But it was for the best. How could he ever look at her again without remembering what he'd done?

She'd accused him of being high-handed and arrogant. Why couldn't she understand that unlike the last time he'd left her, he was leaving her for her own good this time?

When his phone rang, he was sprawled in his easy chair thinking about her because he was unable to focus on his business journal or the television. Thankful for any diversion, he grabbed the receiver.

"Mr. Pierre, he be gone," Noonoon said in a worried tone.

"What?" He grabbed his remote and punched Mute.

"I tried to get you earlier, only I got a message saying you had your phone turned off."

"Sorry about that. I've been doing some thinking. What about Grandpère?"

"Mr. Pierre, he been in bad mood ever since he read the paper and had breakfast with Miss Cici. She told him she would be going away. After that nobody could console him. Not even me. So, he be gone. Mr. Jake, he come as soon as I called him."

Why in the hell had he turned his phone off?

"Mr. Jake and Miss Cici and Mr. Bos, they be in the swamp in Mr. Bos's boat looking for him."

"I'll be there as fast as I can," Logan said. Slamming the phone down, he jumped to his feet.

Dressing hurriedly he tore out of his bedroom, down the stairs, taking them two at a time. Then he was outside his mansion, storming blindly to his Lexus.

A cool, cloaking mist was seeping up from the swamp, shrouding everything. There was no wind, no movement of any kind.

Cici felt cramped, hemmed in.

"Pierre?" she called, her heart hammering as the swirls of fog wiped out familiar landmarks.

She hated the damp this evening, hated the way everything was so still and gave off the dank odor of rotting vegetation. Uneasiness swept her. Pierre wasn't strong. She was no longer sure where she was on the plantation, so how could she possibly help Pierre? Would he venture this far into the swamp?

The last of the sunlight was almost gone, but, at least, the evening was still fairly warm. So, maybe he wouldn't be too cold despite the damp. Still, the thought of him walking in this mist, especially after it grew dark, filled her with dread.

Their search party had split up hours ago, so Cici was alone as she picked her way through the dense forest made up of blooming dogwood and tupelo gum as well as cypress and oak at the northern edge of the Claiborne property.

"Pierre?" Her voice sounded soft and fearful even to her own ears, muffled as it was by the mist.

Off to the right she heard a twig pop as if stepped on by a heavy boot, and she jumped.

"Pierre?" Her voice cracked. "Is that you?" Please, God, let it be Pierre.

There was a long silence. Then another twig broke, this one nearer than the first.

"Pierre!" she cried.

"No, it's me, Cici," Logan said, his voice deep and cold.

"Logan…" Relief swamped her.

She almost ran to him before she remembered he'd deliberately rejected her, just like he had before. Freezing, she stood her ground even though the mere sound of his hard, strained voice made her feel as if chains that had bound her heart ever since he'd walked out on her were falling away.

"Where are you?" she said.

"Stay where you are," he commanded. She heard crunching footsteps. Then he stepped out of the fog, but no joy of recognition or love lit his tense, blue eyes.

She drew a deep breath in an attempt to fortify herself.

"I'm sorry about Pierre," she whispered. "This is all my fault. He hasn't been the same since I told him I was leaving."

"I tried to call you."

"But my phone was turned off." His bleak eyes held

no light as he stared through her. "Like always. I'm never there when you need me."

She felt the final death of something in his low tone and couldn't bring herself to reply.

"We'll find him," Logan said but in a heavy, dull voice that didn't cheer her. "This isn't the first time he's pulled a stunt like this. He always just reappears, almost as if by magic, from his wanderings. Usually…he turns up…right before dark. I think the old fellow has a healthy respect for the dark, or maybe he's being considerate of us. He's not that far gone that he doesn't know exactly what he's doing."

"He wants his way, and I can't blame him."

"Still, it's one of the reasons I wanted to move him to New Orleans. His little disappearances always scare everybody half to death—me included."

She swallowed. "I'm sorry that I didn't consider this possibility. Noonoon had told me about the other times."

"When will you leave?"

"In a week."

"So, you have plenty of time to prepare and pack," he said indifferently. Then he turned. "Maybe we should head back to the house just to make sure he hasn't come home already. Like I said, he doesn't like being out after dark much."

Sure enough, everybody, including Pierre and Jake, was on the porch drinking hot tea and laughing when they returned.

"Can I pour you a cup, Mr. Logan, yes?" Noonoon

asked, a smile in her voice now that the crisis was over, and she saw Logan with Cici.

"I'm afraid I have to get back to New Orleans," Logan said curtly as he shook his head. Turning on his heel, he strode off into the darkness in the direction of his car.

Everybody began chattering anew, and Pierre seemed very happy to be home safely and to find himself the center of attention after his misadventure.

All Cici could hear were Logan's footsteps dying away on the gravel path.

"Stubborn, high-handed idiot," Jake muttered, slamming his teacup down. "Some things never change."

She'd told Jake about her misunderstanding with Logan earlier, and he'd told her that Butler had, at least, been lying when he'd said Logan intended to marry his daughter.

When she could no longer hear even Logan's footsteps, pain clogged her throat. He was still stubbornly set against her.

He'd said he was walking out on her for her sake, but to her it felt like history was repeating itself. He was leaving her, and she couldn't bear it. And he didn't care.

Jake leaned toward her. "What are you waiting for? It's obvious you're both miserable. Go after him. He loves you. He's always loved you."

"And you know this how? You've barely spoken these past nine years."

"I still know," he said. "He thinks he's protecting

you. He's hell on wheels when he's protecting one of us. I should be the one to know. Don't let him drive you away, the way I did."

As suddenly as she had when she'd been a child and had seen Logan disappearing into the woods or swamp, she gave a little cry and began to run after him, slowly at first and then more swiftly.

"Logan!"

He didn't answer.

"Logan, wait!"

His legs were longer than hers and he'd had a head start, so he had already reached his Lexus by the time she caught up to him.

"Logan. I love you. Don't leave me, or you'll hurt me more than anything you've ever done before. I love you and I'll be miserable forever if you walk out on me."

He was about to open his door, but when she said his name and then said she loved him in such a breathless rush, he paused.

"You couldn't possibly love me."

"Do you love me?"

"Yes. I love you."

"So, why are you hell-bent on breaking both our hearts?"

"I thought it was for the best."

"For whom? What gives you the right to always make decisions for both of us? Being a couple means you listen to each other and make a decision together that's best for the couple as a unit."

Suddenly she couldn't trust herself to go on. What if he remained dead set against her?

Biting her bottom lip, she felt like her life hung in the balance as she stood there, waiting, hoping that he would change his mind about their future.

"I do love you," he said. "So much…that what I did seems unforgivable."

"Love can forgive anything."

"Can it?"

"In this case. It's my heart. I should be the one to know."

"But I don't deserve you."

"Don't…say that ever again…" She went up to him and silenced his lips with a fingertip. "Kiss me," she said. "Hold me. These last few hours without you have been such hell."

"What about Egypt?"

"I was running away for your sake more than mine this time. Now…there's no reason to go…and every reason…I think…to stay."

"I love you. You do belong in my life. You've always belonged. I was just too blind to see it."

"And you were blinding yourself again to how much I love you and have always loved you."

"My love," he said.

"After I saw your ravaged face in that newspaper photograph after Noelle's death…from that moment I think I wanted to come home. You've suffered enough."

"Hopefully I've finally learned something in the process."

She smiled. "I'm sure of it." But in the next breath she was in his arms, clinging to him tightly, feeling renewed faith in tomorrow and in the day after tomorrow.

Tears of happiness and relief overflowed in her eyes. Once more the future was bright with shared dreams and goals and in the dazzle of all the mutually shared adventures they would have.

"I thought you deserved a better man than me," he said.

"And you always do what's best for those you love on your own, don't you?"

"I try. But this time I didn't know how I'd live without you. I really didn't."

"Me, either. It's scary to think that if Pierre hadn't disappeared, we were both so stubborn set on our path, we might have never had another chance together."

"So I owe him even more than I already did." He looked down at her, his face wide open, his blue eyes filled with love and yet with pain and fear too that he'd come so close to losing her again.

Logan bent his head and buried his face in her hair. She felt the warmth of his lips on her scalp as he wrapped his arms around her and hung on to her as if she meant everything to him.

"You're going to have to be careful about protecting the family from now on," she teased.

"So my best trait…is my worst trait."

"Only sometimes."

"Oh, Cici," he whispered. "My darling…"

"Logan," she murmured in a tone that was equally

passionate. "Logan, I've never been this happy, not even when we began, not even when you first said you loved me. I love you. I love you so much."

He caught her hand, laced his fingers through hers. "Then marry me," he whispered against her ear. "Tomorrow. Or at least as fast as possible. We've wasted way too much time already."

Instead of answering him with words, she reached up and kissed his lips which were hot and hard as they hungrily devoured hers, demanding everything and more that she had to give. Her heart was pounding as he crushed her closer.

Wrapping his arms around her, he began to lead her to the *garçonnière*.

"Shouldn't we tell everybody that we've made up?" she asked.

"All in good time," he said. "I've put you through hell again, so, first, I have to make it up to you."

Cici's warm body lay mashed beneath Logan's on the same bed in the *garçonnière* where they'd first made love. His manhood was deeply embedded inside her. This time he wore no condom because she'd said, "I want another child."

Spirals of her wiry gold hair fanned out on his pillow.

How he loved lying like this with her, body to body, the two of them locked together as if they were one being. He loved the softness of her skin, her velvet voice, her smell. In a lifetime, he would never get enough of her.

For as long as Logan could remember she was all he'd ever wanted; the wild hair, her dark eyes alight with sexual mischief, the slim voluptuous body and even the legs wrapped so tightly around his waist.

Her womb quivered, causing his heart to race even faster. What if she was already carrying his baby?

"Well, go on. What are you waiting for?" she teased in a low whisper.

"You didn't say whether or not you'd marry me."

"Oh, that," she said playfully even as her warm, sparkling eyes made more than enough promises to make his heart overflow with bright, shining hope.

"If I want your baby, marriage definitely goes with the territory."

Epilogue

Everybody from the bad news bikers with their tats and piercings from T-Bos's Bar to the richest and most elegant lords of the bayou in the county came to the Claiborne wedding ceremony which was held at Belle Rose under a big white tent set up at the edge of the swamp. Alicia clung to Jake's arm and watched an unsmiling Bos give his niece, Cici, away to the grandson of his ancient enemy.

Hayes Daniels was the best man, and Noonoon was the matron of honor.

Maybe the guests all came because nobody believed Logan Claiborne would really stand up to his side of the bargain and marry Cici Bellefleur.

But marry her he did, and with such a hot look on his tanned face that every man there knew the groom couldn't wait for the formalities to be over and for his honeymoon to begin.

No, nobody, not even Pierre missed the love and passion in the bride and groom's eyes when the wedding march began in earnest.

Nor did anybody fail to note that the brightly smiling Cici, with demure white roses in her hair, wore a shockingly short white mini skirt and five-inch stilettos as she joined Logan at the altar. What kind of wife would she make such a man, some wondered.

Then the ceremony was over far too quickly, and the groom kissed his bride far too long and much too passionately, because the rest of the world, even his wedding guests, had ceased to exist and did not matter to him at all.

*Bestselling author Lynne Graham is back
with a fabulous new trilogy!*

PREGNANT BRIDES

Three ordinary girls—naive, but also honest and plucky...

*Three fabulously wealthy, impossibly handsome
and very ruthless men...*

*When opposites attract and passion leads to pregnancy...
it can only mean marriage!*

*Available next month from Harlequin Presents®:
the first installment*

DESERT PRINCE, BRIDE OF INNOCENCE

* * *

'THIS EVENING I'm flying to New York for two weeks,'
Jasim imparted with a casualness that made her heart sink
like a stone. 'That's why I had you brought here. I own this
apartment and you'll be comfortable here while I'm abroad.'

'I can afford my own accommodation although I may not
need it for long. I'll have another job by the time you
get back—'

Jasim released a slightly harsh laugh. 'There's no need for
you to look for another position. How would I ever see you?
Don't you understand what I'm offering you?'

Elinor stood very still. 'No, I must be incredibly thick
because I haven't quite worked out yet what you're offering
me....'

His charismatic smile slashed his lean dark visage.
'Naturally, I want to take care of you....'

'No, thanks.' Elinor forced a smile and mentally willed him not to demean her with some sordid proposition. 'The only man who will ever take *care* of me with my agreement will be my husband. I'm willing to wait for you to come back but I'm not willing to be kept by you. I'm a very independent woman and what I give, I give freely.'

Jasim frowned. 'You make it all sound so serious.'

'What happened between us last night left pure chaos in its wake. Right now, I don't know whether I'm on my head or my heels. I'll stay for a while because I have nowhere else to go in the short term. So maybe it's good that you'll be away for a while.'

Jasim pulled out his wallet to extract a card. 'My private number,' he told her, presenting her with it as though it was a precious gift, which indeed it was. Many women would have done just about anything to gain access to that direct hotline to him, but his staff guarded his privacy with scrupulous care.

Before he could close the wallet, his blood ran cold in his veins. How could he have made such a serious oversight? What if he had got her pregnant? He knew that an unplanned pregnancy would engulf his life like an avalanche, crush his freedom and suffocate him. He barely stilled a shudder at the threat of such an outcome and thought how ironic it was that what his older brother had longed and prayed for to secure the line to the throne should strike Jasim as an absolute disaster....

* * *

What will proud Prince Jasim do if Elinor is expecting his royal baby? Perhaps an arranged marriage is the only solution! But will Elinor agree? Find out in DESERT PRINCE, BRIDE OF INNOCENCE by Lynne Graham [#2884], available from Harlequin Presents® in January 2010.

REQUEST YOUR FREE BOOKS!

2 FREE NOVELS
PLUS 2
FREE GIFTS!

Passionate, Powerful, Provocative!

YES! Please send me 2 FREE Silhouette Desire® novels and my 2 FREE gifts (gifts are worth about $10). After receiving them, if I don't wish to receive any more books, I can return the shipping statement marked "cancel". If I don't cancel, I will receive 6 brand-new novels every month and be billed just $4.05 per book in the U.S. or $4.74 per book in Canada. That's a savings of almost 15% off the cover price! It's quite a bargain! Shipping and handling is just 50¢ per book.* I understand that accepting the 2 free books and gifts places me under no obligation to buy anything. I can always return a shipment and cancel at any time. Even if I never buy another book, the two free books and gifts are mine to keep forever.

225 SDN EYMS 326 SDN EYM4

Name	(PLEASE PRINT)	
Address		Apt. #
City	State/Prov.	Zip/Postal Code

Signature (if under 18, a parent or guardian must sign)

Mail to the **Silhouette Reader Service**:
IN U.S.A.: P.O. Box 1867, Buffalo, NY 14240-1867
IN CANADA: P.O. Box 609, Fort Erie, Ontario L2A 5X3

Not valid to current subscribers of Silhouette Desire books.

Want to try two free books from another line?
Call 1-800-873-8635 or visit www.morefreebooks.com.

* Terms and prices subject to change without notice. Prices do not include applicable taxes. Sales tax applicable in N.Y. Canadian residents will be charged applicable provincial taxes and GST. Offer not valid in Quebec. This offer is limited to one order per household. All orders subject to approval. Credit or debit balances in a customer's account(s) may be offset by any other outstanding balance owed by or to the customer. Please allow 4 to 6 weeks for delivery. Offer available while quantities last.

Your Privacy: Silhouette Books is committed to protecting your privacy. Our Privacy Policy is available online at www.eHarlequin.com or upon request from the Reader Service. From time to time we make our lists of customers available to reputable third parties who may have a product or service of interest to you. If you would prefer we not share your name and address, please check here. ☐

SDES09R

COMING NEXT MONTH
Available January 12, 2010

#1987 FROM PLAYBOY TO PAPA!—Leanne Banks
Man of the Month
Surprised to learn he has a son, he's even more surprised to learn his ex-lover's sister is raising the boy. When he demands the child live with him, he agrees to let her come too…as his wife.

#1988 BOSSMAN'S BABY SCANDAL—Catherine Mann
Kings of the Boardroom
What's an executive to do when his one-night stand is pregnant and his new client hates scandal? Propose a temporary marriage, of course. Yet their sizzling passion is anything but temporary….

#1989 TEMPTING THE TEXAS TYCOON—Sara Orwig
He'll receive five million dollars if he marries within the year—and a sexy business rival provides the perfect opportunity. But she refuses to submit to his desires…especially when she discovers his reasons.

**#1990 AFFAIR WITH THE REBEL HEIRESS—
Emily McKay**
Known for his conquests in the boardroom—and the bedroom—the CEO isn't about to let his latest fling stand in his way. He'll acquire her company, wild passion or not. Though he soon finds out she has other plans in mind….

**#1991 THE MAGNATE'S PREGNANCY PROPOSAL—
Sandra Hyatt**
She came to tell him the in vitro worked—she was carrying his late brother's baby. When he drops the bomb that her baby is actually *his,* he'll stop at nothing to stake his claim. Will she let him claim *her?*

#1992 CLAIMING HIS BOUGHT BRIDE—Rachel Bailey
To meet the terms of his inheritance, he convinces her to marry him. But can he seduce her into being his wife more than just on paper?